WILLOW BROOKE

AJ WYNN

First paperback edition March 2024

Cover designed by: Halle with AJ Wolf Graphics
Formatting by: Halle with AJ Wolf Graphics
Floor plan CAD design by: Termeh Studio
Edited by: Sam Willow
Proofread by: EF Watson

eBook ISBN 979-8-9895960-0-3
Paperback ISBN 979-8-9895960-1-0

www.AJWynn.com

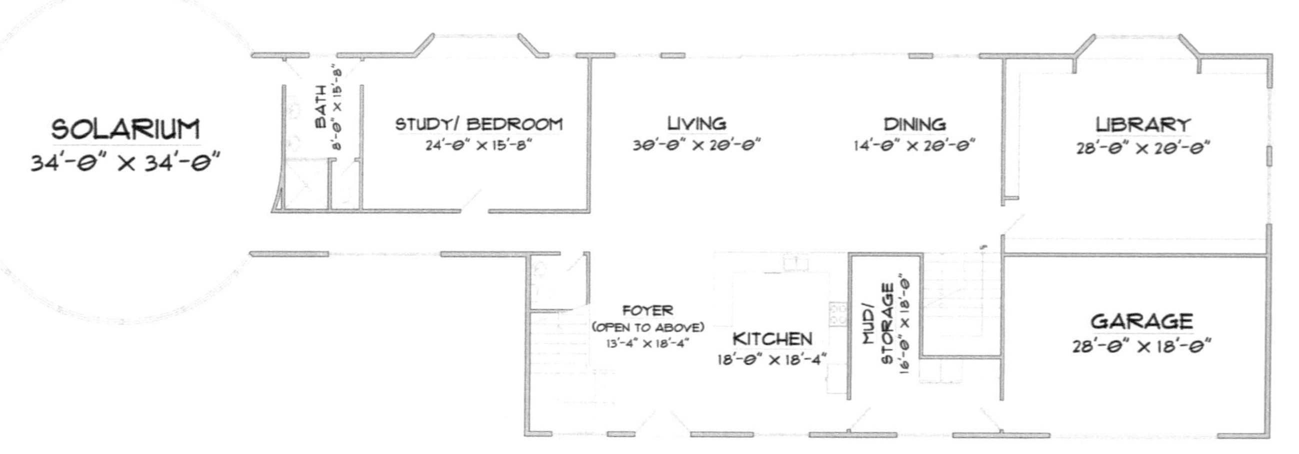

FIRST FLOOR PLAN
1/4"= 1'-0"

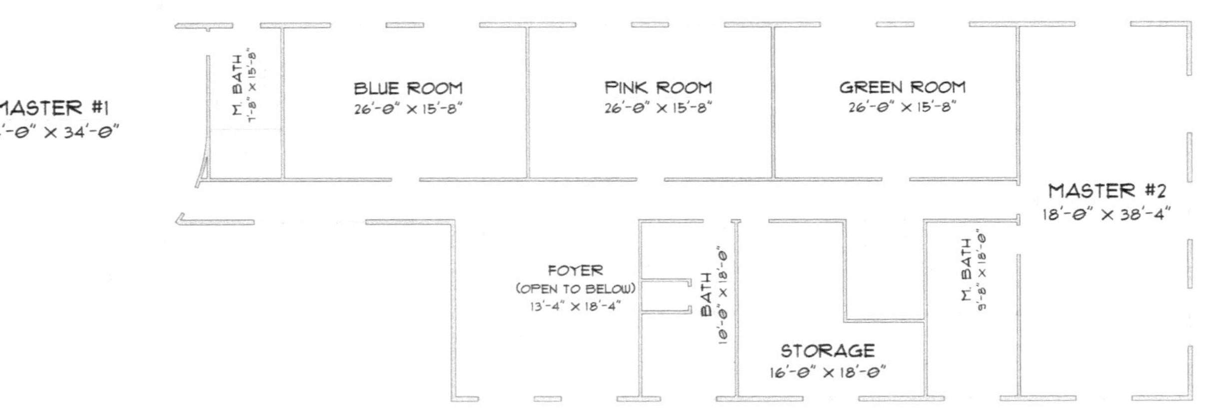

MASTER #1
34'-0" X 34'-0"
M. BATH
7'-8" X 15'-8"
BLUE ROOM
26'-0" X 15'-8"
PINK ROOM
26'-0" X 15'-8"
GREEN ROOM
26'-0" X 15'-8"
MASTER #2
18'-0" X 38'-4"
FOYER
(OPEN TO BELOW)
13'-4" X 18'-4"
BATH
10'-0" X 18'-0"
STORAGE
16'-0" X 18'-0"
M. BATH
9'-8" X 18'-0"
SECOND FLOOR PLAN
1/4"= 1'-0"

For my biggest cheerleader and best friend,
my mom. ♥

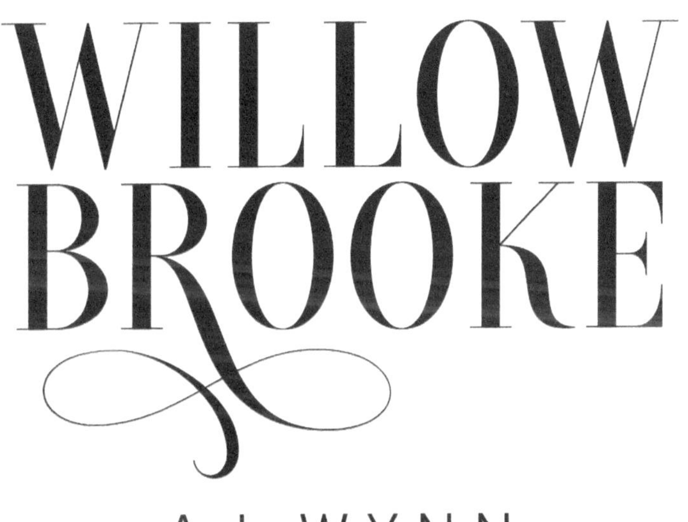

WILLOW BROOKE

AJ WYNN

This isn't a ghost story.

But it's kind of a ghost story.

I guess it depends on how you define ghosts…

But when I first saw Willowbrooke, I definitely remember thinking, *This place is for sure haunted.*

And it absolutely was.

CHAPTER 1

THE JOB

"My life is over, Mina." I sniffled into the phone.

"Penny…" Mina sighed. "You knew going in this wasn't going to be an easy task, but you tried anyway. That's what's important."

Mina, ever the optimist and my perpetual hype-girl, was trying her hardest to build me back up, which was precisely why I had called her in the first place. But I was feeling so low, I wasn't ready to stop wallowing just yet.

"Perhaps I can find a career in constant failure," I lamented. "Failed architect. Failed daughter. Failed independent person. Failed girlfriend."

"Listen, I know things aren't going how you want them

to right now—"

"What? The part about me being thirty-three, with no career, an emotionally unavailable boyfriend, and absolutely nothing to look forward to?" I grumbled.

"Penny, this shit takes time." Mina's voice became more firm. "Everyone's journey is different, and yeah, maybe you accidentally turned on hard mode, but that doesn't mean you won't come out of this alive.

"All these perceived failures are part of your story. You need to fail once in a while to help you understand how things work, to learn life lessons, and to eliminate what's not working for you.

"Even if you had gone through with the architecture degree to make Mommy and Daddy happy, and tried to live up to the impossible standards your sister set, you'd be pleasing them at your own expense, while you wasted away in a job you hated. I was with you during college—you HATED those architecture classes. It was never going to work. You cannot please them, you need to work toward finding your own happiness."

"When I brought you this lead, I warned you. I told you that he passed on all the big firms and local talent. I said it was a long shot, but it would at least give you a reason to put together your portfolio."

I cringed, recalling the slim folder I had, in my haste, left on the kitchen counter. I had been so proud of it before I'd set foot in that house, but I'd left feeling humiliated by it.

"It was meant to be a way for you to get a taste of interviewing and pitching to clients. And if it worked out, great, but if not, then on to the next."

I knew she was right, but I'd built it up in my head as this end all, be all, last hope kinda project to start forging my own path away from the firm. I knew I was out of my depth with the scope of the project, given my lack of experience, but I'd let myself hope, and yet again, I found myself so incredibly disappointed by the results.

"You have to be exaggerating how badly it went. I love you, but you tend to be hyperbolic. Tell me exactly what happened—the facts, no more woe-is-me rhetoric."

Reluctantly, I began to recall the events of the last few hours in painful detail.

Pulling up to Willowbrooke took my breath away.

The stunning, shingle-style home was more of a manor or mansion than a house. Sitting on twenty acres, the seven-bedroom, four-and-a-half bath home boasted a sprawling back lawn that led to a cliffside overlooking the ocean, with private beach access, a three-bedroom, two-bath guest cottage, and privacy from all sides, due to the willow trees dotting and lining the property.

It was so well hidden, in fact, that I had almost missed the turnoff for the long driveway that allowed access to the property, nestled beyond the front grove of willow trees.

It had taken me over an hour and a half commute from the city to the house, which was a half hour longer than I had anticipated, but I was still thirty minutes early. I'd been terrified to arrive late, so I'd added a generous buffer to quell my ever-present anxiety.

From where I was parked at the edge of the driveway, I hoped I wouldn't be as noticeable to anyone looking out from inside the house. While I felt it was always good to be early, it could be perceived as rude to show up early and not introduce oneself, but a half hour was also much too early to risk catching Mr. West off guard.

It was imperative that I make a positive first impression.

Interior design had long been my passion, but I had been derailed in the pursuit of those dreams by a handful of factors. While I had an associate's degree in the field, I'd been sidelined working as an office manager at my parent's architecture firm for the past decade.

While I applied to jobs in my field and helped friends in exchange for pictures I could use in my portfolio, I hadn't had professional success in my preferred career. I had all but given up on the idea, until Mina had told me about the project that had the city's designers abuzz.

At first we'd only joked about how, firm by firm, designer by designer, the mysterious Mr. West was rejecting proposals, running through all his potential options.

And then out of the blue, Mina suggested I throw my hat into the ring. "Maybe what Mr. West needs is a fresh perspective—and that's exactly what you offer." She smiled at me over coffee one Saturday morning.

It was a huge risk, but I had nothing to lose.

Slightly tipsy after a couple mimosas, I submitted an interview request and was surprised when less than an hour later, Mr. West replied with a date and time.

With Mina's help, I put together the best portfolio I could manage. She suggested I offer to provide both design and project management services. While I wasn't sure I could handle all the duties, Mina argued my work at the firm proved otherwise, as I often jumped in to help with admin tasks that she considered more project coordination, and that offering to do both jobs would differentiate me, and could allow me to go full-time on the project and quit the firm.

The thought of leaving the firm was equally terrifying and exhilarating, but still one that kept me very motivated to secure the contract.

With five minutes to go until our scheduled interview time, I got out of the car, adjusted my blazer, and checked my makeup in the driver-side window. I attempted to tame some flyaways, before tucking my portfolio under my arm, and marching across the gravel driveway to the front door—not an easy task in heels, especially when I rarely wore anything other than my favorite pair of white sneakers, that could *just* pass for professional work attire.

The exterior was pristine, even if, in the gloomy weather, the house looked both formidable and somewhat oppressive.

Upon closer inspection, I noticed small signs of neglect, previous exterior renovations which had not only been poorly executed and maintained, but that had also compromised the integrity of the original design elements. But the damage I could see was only from the last few decades, as it seemed the home had been well-loved and maintained prior to that.

I wondered if the outside was within scope of what Mr. West had wanted to accomplish. As it was already late August, nothing could likely be done to the outside until spring, and it would stretch the project out quite longer than I had initially anticipated.

Taking a deep breath, I stepped up to the massive wood double doors and used the knocker to announce myself. The heavy door creaked gently as it swung open a moment later.

I visibly gulped when I first laid eyes on the mysterious and persnickety Mr. West, who couldn't have been much older than myself, much to my shock. Mina and I had frequently joked over the past couple weeks about what kind of shrewd, stodgy blue blood he would be.

But Leo West didn't seem to be any of those things.

He was quite handsome, with perhaps an air of melancholy about him.

Standing tall in a crisp white button-down, with the top two buttons undone casually, sleeves rolled up to his elbows, and the hem tucked into his well-fitting black slacks, he left me speechless.

I don't know exactly what I had been expecting, but it

wasn't him.

"Mr. West?" I questioned, robotically sticking my hand out to shake his.

"Leo, please." He gave me a tight smile, assessing me as he shook my hand.

"I'm Penny Abbot," I replied, feeling like the sound of my own voice was foreign, far away, and small.

"Please, come in." Leo stepped back, allowing me room to cross the threshold into the foyer.

I couldn't help but let my eyes linger on the flexed muscles of his forearm as I slipped past him, avoiding eye contact and trying desperately to ignore the sudden flutter of a foreign feeling in my belly. Was it nerves, excitement…attraction?

"Welcome to Willowbrooke," he said evenly, closing the door behind me.

I was immediately overwhelmed as my senses went into overdrive. I didn't know where to focus my attention. A flurry of dust assaulted my allergies, momentarily distracting me.

Squinting to see past the dim light of the foyer, I was surprised that all the curtains in the home were drawn, making the gloomy morning appear more like dusk. The air was thick with the smell of disinfectant, immediately making me feel like I was in a hospital.

I remembered Mina had told me while doing research on Mr. West—Leo—for her firm, that his father had passed away recently, which she suspected was the impetus for the project, and would explain the melancholy.

"You have a beautiful home," I fumbled, trying to say something that would fill the silence. My tone might have come across as disingenuous, but I saw the potential all around me.

A grand staircase to my left led up to the second floor, and one of the past renovations had knocked down a good chunk of the interior walls, leaving the kitchen, on my right, completely open to a large living room and dining room space beyond.

If the curtains had been opened, it would have offered a stunning view of the cliffside and ocean behind the house. Absently I thought that I might be able to find old records of the original blueprints filed with the city, which would help with any required restoration.

In a rare moment of candor, Leo raked his hand through his hair, mussing it more than it had already been. The action seemed bashful. "It needs a lot of work," he sighed. "Do you want a tour?"

I nodded and followed behind Leo as he escorted me out of the foyer. "The solarium and my bedroom are down that hall." He pointed to the left, past the main staircase. "No work is required in either space." He led me through the open living and kitchen space without providing any additional notes.

A sectional sofa that was too small for the space, upholstered with a ruffled floral fabric that was at least twenty years old, was the only place to sit in the living room.

It faced the hopefully original fireplace, with a chunky, chipped wood coffee table standing guard between the two. Off in the corner was a bulky, squat TV stand, with a TV that was almost as large and almost as square, bowing the particle board on which it sat.

In contrast, behind the living room was a beautiful vintage dining table, with eight dining chairs neatly arranged around the curves of the table legs. That would definitely be staying, but it would have looked much more stately in natural light and with a fresh floral arrangement in the center.

Opening a door at the end of the room, he extended his arm, encouraging me to proceed before him. "The library."

Again, the room was devoid of natural light. "Can I open the curtains?" I asked.

"No," Leo replied flatly.

I nodded, giving no indication of my confusion at his ambivalence. Strangely, despite the lack of lighting, the sprawling space was like something out of a book.

Leo led me up a narrow staircase, likely used by servants when the home was first built in the eighteen hundreds.

The second floor was warmer and even more stifling than the first. I followed Leo room by room. He quickly opened and closed doors for the dual masters on either side of the home, the three modestly-sized bedrooms in between them, and the bathrooms.

The three guest rooms would have had views overlooking the back lawn, out to the ocean, if the windows had been open. Each decorated in a different color. One in green, one in pink, and one in blue.

Sheets covered most of the furniture in the rooms, leaving me eager to uncover what gems might lie beneath. The more authentic and vintage pieces that could be reused in the home, the better.

"Will you require redecorating for all the rooms?" I asked, trying again, awkwardly, to make conversation.

"Yes, they haven't been touched for almost thirty years." Leo paused, "I don't know what's in all the rooms. Do you require an inventory?" For the first time since he'd opened the front door, he made eye contact with me.

His gaze was dark and deep. The intensity caused my stomach to flutter.

I looked away as I shook my head. "Not right away, just curious—if there are quality pieces, it would be great to keep them here."

Leo didn't respond. He merely closed the door to the second master and turned to make his way back down the grand staircase at the front of the house, bringing us back to the foyer yet again. Leo continued into the kitchen, pulling out a barstool at the counter for me, before taking a seat next to me.

A pregnant pause added to the stagnant air before I decided to speak first, rather than wait for Leo, who seemed lacking in conversation. "Here's my portfolio." I slid the binder across the counter toward him.

Leo pushed it to the side and made eye contact with me again. "So, what would you do with the house?" he asked plainly.

I took a beat; this wasn't how I had expected the interview to start. "I think the better question is what do *you* want to do with the house?" I replied. "Your needs, tastes, and desires are what should drive a project this big."

Leo narrowed his gaze for a split second, and I thought perhaps I had annoyed him with my answer. "If it was *yours*, what would you do?" he rephrased his question.

I leaned back on the stool, breaking eye contact to refocus on the open living space behind him. "Well, all the curtains would be open, first of all. The natural lighting, with the positioning of the home, would completely change the vibe of the place."

Leo seemed to consider my request, but didn't move a muscle.

I continued, "I can see there was a larger scale renovation done around the eighties, if I had to guess. The workmanship, both inside and outside is less than spectacular—maybe a bit too trendy for the time. It doesn't adequately showcase the original features of the home." I looked around, wrinkling my nose at the faux wood paneling behind the dining set.

"Even if the curtains were open, it's much too dark in here. There's a time and place for a moodier room—the library, for instance, looks beautiful with darker tones, but this space"—I used my arms to motion around me—"it could and should be lighter.

"The rooms upstairs—what I could see of them, are also dated, but there seems to be a lot of vintage, perhaps even original furniture around the house." I paused. "If the house was mine, I would restore what I could—this style of home is quintessential New England, and the damage done by the past renovations can be fixed.

"I think there's a way to marry the original work with a mix of vintage and modern furnishings and textiles, while paying homage to the original design. You don't have to sacrifice modern conveniences or aesthetics to do this home justice."

I gave Leo a moment to respond; he remained silent, but I thought perhaps he was intrigued.

I continued, "There are big jobs to be done here. The flooring will need to be replaced, but under the linoleum and carpet, there may be original hardwood floors. There are details missing that should be present in a home this age, but there are good reproductions available now, so it would be easy to undo the mistakes made by past changes."

I smiled at Leo, indicating I was finished, and he nodded.

He pulled my portfolio in front of him and began to flip through it. The light that I thought I'd seen in his eyes while I had described what I could do for his home slowly faded.

I held back a sigh, preparing myself for what was coming next.

"An associate's degree," he stated.

I nodded, though he was still focused on the folder in front of him. "Yes, and my experience at Abbot Architecture for the last decade makes me uniquely qualified to handle project management as well." I repeated verbatim what Mina had instructed me to say.

Leo glanced up at me. "You'd do both?"

"Yes." I nodded again.

His eyes returned to the portfolio. "You don't have any professional experience with your design work, just small projects?" He seemed unimpressed with the photos of the apartment living rooms—I had known he would be.

"No, but interior design is my passion, and I know this is a big project, so I think I can give you a fresh perspective, and I would be completely dedicated to this job." I swallowed the lump in my throat and blinked back the tears I could feel welling in my eyes.

I didn't believe a word I was saying, and Leo knew it.

"I would really love to help you bring this house back to life." I managed to make eye contact with him for a moment, as I'd meant those last few words.

Leo closed the portfolio. Seeing it on the counter under his large hand made it look even thinner than I remembered. "I have a lot to consider," he replied.

"I see." I understood what he was getting at. I figured I'd save him the time of telling me that he'd let me know, and save myself the sting of rejection that would follow. "Thank you for your time." I stood from the barstool and put my hand out to shake his once more.

He reluctantly returned the gesture, brow furrowed. "Would you like to leave a business card?"

I paused, embarrassed. "I don't have one." I blinked back more tears; I couldn't cry in front of him or I would be even more mortified than I already was. "All my contact information is in my portfolio." I winced at the shakiness in my voice. "Thank you," I mumbled once again, before turning on my heel and walking back through the front door. I managed to make it to my car before crumbling completely.

I felt so foolish for putting so much hope on this project and allowing myself to dream about what it would be like to start this career I'd been trying desperately to pursue for years. I wanted to know what it would feel like to finally prove to my parents that this field was good enough...that *I* was good enough...

Watching Leo while I'd described what I could see for the house, I could have sworn I had seen a spark there—that he'd seen what I had, that my vision could be his too, but then I'd ruined it because I hadn't been able to back it up with experience.

I'd been applying to a few firms, including the one where Mina worked, but nobody wanted to hire someone my age with my lack of experience. Even though I said I was willing to take a pay cut, to start at the bottom, they wanted fresh faces and designers right out of school for their entry level positions—easily moldable and trainable.

Without experience, I couldn't hope to work for a design firm, and without experience at a design firm, I couldn't hope to get freelance work.

I was stuck.

My dream was dead.

I was hopeless.

Knowing she would be expecting my call, I decided to rip the Band-Aid off and talk to Mina right away. At least she'd give me a sorely-needed pep talk.

And she sure did.

"You're too hard on yourself." Mina sighed after I finished recounting my sorry tale. "And you shouldn't have left before he asked you to—you cut him off, what if he had more questions—you made assumptions and ran away," she accused me, and rightfully so.

"It's better this way," I tried to reframe my disappointment. "The commute is terrible from the city, the house is gorgeous, but creepy as fuck—definitely haunted." That earned a giggle from Mina. "And Leo—he's impossible to read—no wonder he can't find a good fit. Are you sure they didn't turn him down? He doesn't even know what he wants."

Mina's melodious laughter filled the phone receiver. "Seriously!? Who wants to do a total renovation without having a clue about what they want to change? And what was up with all the curtains being drawn? Maybe he's a vampire," she joked.

I joined her giggling, but paused when my phone began

to vibrate in my hand. I pulled it away from my ear.

"Mina!" I stopped her. "He's calling me!? What should I do? He's probably calling to tell me I didn't get it—doesn't want to draw it out, right?" My heart hammered.

Mina continued to laugh. "Answer it, silly. Call me back when you're done."

I switched over to the other line and tried my best to sound professional. "Penny Abbot."

"You left before we discussed salary and time frames." Leo's brooding tone slipped through the phone.

"I'm sorry—I didn't realize—I thought we were done," I stuttered.

Leo didn't reply, so I set to answering his question about the project length.

"I would expect the interiors to take a minimum of four to six months, but we'd have to get an inspection done to see if there is any unseen damage that needs to be fixed during the process, in order to keep the home well maintained."

"You didn't have your rates listed in your portfolio. I assume they are standard market value."

"Yes." I nodded dumbly. I had figured out the lowest hourly rate I could survive on, but had planned to let Leo start the salary negotiation because the project was too important to me.

"I assume you'd require an additional monthly retainer to ensure my house is the only project you're working on?" he inquired.

"Yes," I replied without thinking.

A retainer!? I didn't have the experience to expect one, but I wasn't going to tell him that.

"I'll email you the contract right now. If you would like to further negotiate the proposed rates before signing, let me know. How soon can you start?"

"I'd like to give two weeks' notice—would the first of September be okay?" I hoped my quick math was correct on the date.

"Yes."

"Leo," I said before he could hang up, "thank you—I won't let you down." I smiled.

"I'll see you in two weeks," he replied before the call ended.

I pulled up my email and refreshed it until the contract email appeared. I scrolled through the legal disclaimers until I made it to the rates.

I gasped at the numbers. Surely they couldn't be correct. He had to have misplaced a decimal.

What he considered market value was high for a seasoned designer. The retainer was even more impressive. I thought about the student loans I still had to pay off and tried to do some quick math to calculate how much faster I could do so with this salary.

It was all happening so quickly.

Without needing another moment to think, I completed the contract through a link in the email.

It was done. I was an interior designer. I had booked Willowbrooke.

I took a deep breath, then immediately hit redial. "Mina—I got the job!"

CHAPTER 2

IT BEGINS

My last two weeks at the firm were filled with a mix of agonizing days, counting clocks, and waves of anxiety.

It's odd how time can seem to take forever to pass while you're in the midst of it, but afterward feels like it elapsed in the blink of an eye.

I tried to make the best of the time I had because I knew once I started working with Leo at Willowbrooke, things would never be the same. I had taken the leap of faith and was hanging midair, waiting to see if I would land on solid ground or plummet to the depths below.

My parents took the news better than I expected. I

had nightmares about doors slamming and lamps being thrown—not that they were prone to physical outbursts. I knew going into the meeting I had scheduled they could tell something was wrong, as I had never requested a meeting like this before.

"Did Adam propose?" My mom asked, eyes twinkling, looking well put together in a matching navy suit.

"No." My face fell. Why on earth would they think I would call a business meeting to tell them I was engaged? I was pretty sure they would have preferred Adam as a son instead of me as their daughter. "I'm leaving the company," I said quietly.

My dad's brow furrowed, and his hands dropped from the table. "Leaving to go where?"

"I got a job working as an interior designer—it's a huge opportunity—"

"Sweetie," my mom interrupted. She sounded as though she thought I was making it up. "You can't leave us in the lurch like this—what brought this on? We adjusted your salary last year when you hit your ten-year mark with the firm."

Ignoring the fact that it had been over two years since the paltry raise, I slid a paper across the table. "This is my letter of resignation—and my two weeks' notice."

I tried to remain resolute. I could hear Mina in my head: "Don't let them take this from you," she told me.

"I appreciate everything you have done for me, and I've

gained a lot of experience working at the firm, but it's time for me to move on and pursue my own career."

My father shook his head and tried to hide his annoyance. I wasn't a teenager and this wasn't a phase, but they didn't seem to realize that. "Two weeks?" He pursed his lips. "You're blindsiding us like this, and you can only be bothered to give us two weeks to find and train a replacement?"

In a rare moment of courage, I felt compelled to speak my truth, knowing that my life was becoming untethered from my dependance on them. "I've put my dreams on hold for over a decade to help the firm. I wish you would consider supporting my choices and be proud of me for trying to become more independent." I tried to maintain eye contact for as long as I could.

"I will do everything I can to assist with the transition. It's not my intention to cause issues as a result of my departure." I could feel myself begin to tremble, holding back the anger I so desperately wanted to unleash on them. But there was no point in burning the rickety bridge that remained between us. Professionalism and the high ground were my only option.

"I'm disappointed in you." Mom frowned before getting up to leave the room.

"You're sure you know what you're doing?" Dad's eyes narrowed in on me. "If it doesn't work out, I don't know if there will be a place left here for you."

I wasn't sure if that was a threat or meant to be helpful.

"Even if I fail, at least I will have tried." I shrugged, before getting up and leaving the conference room. I had hoped to feel lighter after the meeting, but instead I felt dread over the weeks to come, and their doubt had me second-guessing everything.

The news spread like wildfire through the office.

Adam found me during lunch, eating alone at my desk, like every other day, because nobody else was willing to cover the phones.

Adam was as attractive as he was charming. Just like Leo West, he looked great in a suit, but the similarities between the two stopped there. He prioritized self-care to maintain his good looks, spending time at the tanning salon, dropping more on skincare than my salary at the firm, and making sure every piece of clothing he owned was tailored within an inch of its life.

I supposed he had always been so well put together, but when I had first met Adam, he'd made it seem effortless. After having lived with him for over a year, I'd seen behind the smoke and mirrors, and it often left me wondering if the Adam I knew was truly an authentic version of himself, or a perfectly curated facade he had spent years manufacturing.

Adam vented about feeling left out of the loop. He was understandably upset that I hadn't told him beforehand. But I hadn't trusted that he wouldn't tell my parents before I got the chance, or try to talk me out of it before giving my notice. I couldn't have afforded either transgression, and while things between us remained delicate, I didn't think I could get past a betrayal like that.

I could have, and perhaps should have, stood up for myself and my decisions, but more often, as of late, I found it easier to let him say what he needed to say, rather than arguing my point. I thought Adam just wanted to feel heard and understood, even if I didn't agree with him.

"Penny, I love you," he insisted, squeezing my hand.

I looked up at him hopefully. I wanted him to be happy for me.

"But sometimes you make it hard to take your side."

I felt my shoulders slump in defeat, my gaze falling to the floor.

I didn't think there should be sides to a relationship. I thought we were supposed to be a team. It hadn't felt like that in a while…in fact, I couldn't really think of the last time it had.

"I didn't want to put you in a bad position, Adam," I lied. "This way, you can tell them that you didn't know and didn't have a chance to make me reconsider," I tried to placate him. "Trust me, it'll work out for you better this way. I know they're getting ready to offer you that promotion you've been asking for."

"Honey." He pulled me into a loose hug, softening. "Let's go to dinner tonight to celebrate." He placed a soft kiss at my temple. "I know how big of a deal this is for you."

"Bella Vita?" I asked. It was my favorite restaurant in the area.

"Sure," Adam agreed. He paused for a moment. "But next time…"

"I know, I'm sorry."

At the very least, I had one person firmly in my corner. Mina wasted no time helping me prep ahead of my first day, so I could go in overly prepared for whatever Leo West had to throw at me.

Using some templates she'd stolen from work, we drafted a master plan and proposal for the interior of the property, including an in-depth project timeline. She got a printout of her firm's preferred contractors, under the condition that I not expose who had referred me. And finally, she had notes on all the inspectors to avoid for the project, so I'd be able to schedule an inspection right away, after getting Leo's approval.

"You're going to crush this." Mina smiled across the table at our favorite cafe the Sunday afternoon before my first day. "Don't think about your parents—they'll get over it when they see how amazing you are. This is going to open so many doors for you, and it's only a matter of time before they start taking credit for pushing you to do this." She laughed.

I was ready, or well…I thought I was.

"You drink coffee?" Leo asked quietly while I followed

him to the kitchen.

Seeing him again after our first meeting had my head spinning a bit. He was even more attractive than I remembered. I hated that he made me feel so nervous. Just because he was good-looking and stiffly polite didn't mean that my heart should be pounding in my chest the way it was. I wasn't even available.

I had spent the long commute trying not to psych myself out over what I was about to embark upon and replaying how our original encounter had transpired. I was determined to get more insight into who he was and what he wanted out of this project.

The way he spoke, how he'd regarded me, even his posture demonstrated how on guard he was at all times. I could sense the walls he had erected around himself over a long period of time. I wondered what had happened to him that required such protection. It couldn't just have been the recent loss of his father. I felt myself yearning to comfort him, despite the fact that I barely knew him. I *wanted* to know him.

I remembered laughing at myself in the car, having thought for a moment that maybe we would grow to become friends. I wasn't sure if Leo was even the type of person who could maintain friendships, because if he was as quiet and short with others as he'd been with me, it would have taken someone dogged and determined to be in his life to stick around long enough to see beyond the facade he had up to protect whatever he was hiding beneath the surface.

But Leo's facade felt so different from Adam's. Adam was insecure, but Leo seemed very confident in himself, just private. Although I supposed what they had in common was the need to hide their vulnerabilities. I knew what Adam's were, but I had yet to discover Leo's.

"Definitely—I take it black." I smiled as I answered his query. The awkwardness between us was palpable, but I was determined to get past it. "I've done a ton of prep work to give us a head start, but I was hoping you might let me know exactly what your expectations are for me and the project, so I make sure I'm doing right by you."

Mina had suggested the question about expectations since our arrangement was so loose and I didn't have experience or the backing of a firm to guide me in the process. "Keep Leo West happy, and you'll be fine," Mina had assured me.

Leo's face was blank. "I don't know—I just want everything done to the highest standard." He slid a steaming mug of coffee across the kitchen counter to me.

There was something I had been desperate to ask, and I'd told myself not to, but seeing as I still wasn't clear on his response, I decided to use the opportunity to satisfy my curiosity. "Let me put it to you another way." I bit my lip nervously. "You turned down every firm, every acclaimed designer in the tri-state area—why did you pick me? I'm a nobody—I have no real-world experience, just drive and passion." I chanced a glance up at Leo.

"You shouldn't be so hard on yourself," Leo said quietly,

maybe hoping I hadn't heard him.

Again, I felt my heart flutter. He didn't know me, but he seemed to respect me. I wasn't sure what I had done to earn his respect, but I appreciated that, other than Mina, he was one of few people who had offered me encouragement.

I held my tongue, waiting for him to answer my question. Leo pursed his lips, thinking about how exactly to reply. "You were the only person that asked me what I wanted to do with the space and actually cared about what I said."

"You never did answer the question." I gave a humorless laugh.

"I wanted to collaborate with someone. My answer wasn't the point, the point was that you wanted to work *with* me— you didn't want to tell me what this place should look like and go do it, without another word from me.

"This house is where I grew up. It's belonged to my family for generations. It means something to me." Leo's gaze was firmly on his coffee. It was clear being this open was not easy for him. "I appreciate that this house now means something to you too. Perhaps this project can be a new beginning for both of us."

I nodded in agreement. Our interview had seemed so short, and I was taken aback that he had gotten all of that from our exchange. But more so that he was spot-on. I did care what he thought, and I did want to work alongside him. And of course this project meant everything to me. But I hadn't said that to him…he just understood.

Leo took a sip of his coffee, then paused, debating on saying something else. Finally, he gave in. "And I just..." His eyes met mine, gauging my reaction as he said, "...like you."

I tried not to show it, but I'm sure he observed that I was surprised by his candor. His tone wasn't quite suggestive, but a blush still bloomed across my cheeks.

He sensed something in me—something I didn't see myself. But I knew then that I wanted to prove him right. I wanted to show him that he wouldn't regret giving me a chance. And if he couldn't see my shock at his answer, or the determination it inspired for him, despite the fact that he already seemed to be able to read me so easily, surely my pleased silence said more than enough.

"So, show me your plans," he said.

"First, we have to open the curtains in here—I'm withering without the natural light," I pleaded. "Unless you're allergic to the sun?" I raised a brow in jest.

Leo sighed, but gestured toward the windows, giving me permission to proceed.

"Don't you find it creepy and stuffy in here with them always closed?" I raised my voice to reach him across the room's expanse, while I pulled back panel after panel.

Leo merely shrugged.

"There." I stood back, looking at the stunning view of the back lawn and ocean beyond the cliffside, the room now bathed in natural light. "Isn't that so much better?"

Leo remained impassive.

In the light, Leo's face became more sallow, revealing dark circles under his eyes.

When was the last time he'd slept?

Dressed in an almost identical outfit as when I had first met him, his forearm muscles were more visible in the natural light, as well as the lean lines of his long legs in his impeccably fitted slacks.

"The plans, Penny?" Leo drummed his fingers on the countertop impatiently.

"Right!" I rushed back to the kitchen and pulled a huge stack of documents and binders from my messenger bag.

Leo's eyes widened for a brief moment at the display.

"Okay, so what I'd like to do today is go over the game plan for the next couple weeks." I pulled out an oversized tri-fold I'd had specially printed to show the proposed project timeline.

"You made a Gantt chart?" Leo asked—dare I say— slightly impressed.

I nodded, trying to hide a smile as he pulled the chart across the counter to examine it.

"This week, and maybe into next, depending on how quickly we get through everything, I'd like to go room by room with you to discuss your ideas and my suggestions, so I can create a design for each one—I already have mood boards, but if they aren't to your taste, I can redesign them," I offered, separating out the mood boards from the rest of the documents in a single stack. "I also have all of this online if you prefer soft copies. I used a software where you can add comments, feedback, and make edits, if you'd like."

"Send me the link," Leo said absently, as he began to review the mood boards.

I truly hadn't expected him to be so interested in the designs, but the thought delighted me. While many designers had their own points of view and were hired to impart their vision on a space, I wanted the collaboration that Leo desired as well.

"I'd also like to do a full furniture inventory with you—we can talk about what pieces you like, and if there are any you'd like to get rid of, I can have that arranged."

"That's fine as long as we don't go into the solarium—it's strictly off-limits." His eyes met mine; he needed confirmation that I understood him.

"I remember." I smiled gently, reassuringly.

"Once we've got the broad strokes confirmed," I said, "I'll need to go out and source the materials—do you have any interest in coming with? I wasn't sure what your work schedule is like." Mina and I had speculated about his job, but we'd come up empty.

"I'm not working currently—I'll join you—this project is my only focus right now." Leo took another sip of his coffee.

He'd really meant it when he'd said he wanted to collaborate with me.

It occurred to me that he was probably a trust fund kid, and with his father gone, he'd likely inherited everything. He didn't need to work.

I felt a tinge of envy, but suppressed it. The truth was, I still didn't know anything about Leo West, and it was impolite to make assumptions about him, even if I couldn't help it.

"Great." I smiled up at him again. "I'll be glad to have the company and your opinion." I finished my own coffee then. "Once we've got an idea of lead times on the raw materials, I'll start figuring out when we'll need to book the contractors. I've got some referrals already."

"You mentioned an inspection?" Leo asked.

"Yes!" I dug around for another sheet. "Just to be safe, it would be good to schedule someone right away, so if there are any major issues, we can address them immediately and build anything required into the project timeline and budget." I bit my lip, worried about the next bit. "And you haven't specified a budget yet…that was the only other big thing I wanted to discuss with you." I chanced a glance up at him.

Leo was unfazed. "There isn't one," he said simply.

I nodded at the revelation. I was curious to see, once we actually started shopping for materials, if that stance changed, but until I had a better idea of what he had in mind, I'd keep moving ahead. "So room by room—where do you want to start?"

We made it through all the rooms within the first three days, and started on the much more laborious task of furniture inventory and photography for the next two weeks. Leo surprised me by being rather agreeable to the plans I had put forth.

Getting a solid opinion out of him was like pulling teeth, I learned quickly, so I only dug in and insisted on things that were really important, like how often he actually used the kitchen—he admitted to enjoying cooking quite a bit, which altered my initial plans to be more chef-friendly.

He wouldn't relent on how often he watched TV, but insisted there be one in the living room anyway. He also never used the dining table, but wanted to keep the one he had, right where it was. Luckily, I agreed with him on that. Much to my delight, the hideous floral ruffle sectional in the living room was mutually hated, and he seemed very interested in the updated furniture and floor plan I had proposed.

The library didn't require much beyond a new floor plan and reorganization of the books themselves. Even Leo admitted he didn't know where anything was.

"Mom always kept it organized," he'd mumbled to himself absently, unaware that I had overheard him. It was the first time he'd said anything about her, and it was clear she was no longer in the picture, and hadn't been for a long time.

Upstairs, we thankfully discovered that the decrepit shag carpet in every room was indeed hiding original hardwood floors, as I had expected. "They're herringbone," I'd gushed at the pattern.

"Is that good?" Leo questioned, standing above me.

I sat back on my heels. "It's excellent." I beamed. "And they look to be in good condition, but we won't know for sure until we get all the carpet up."

All of the bedrooms had solid, vintage furniture pieces, but some required reupholstery or minor hardware repairs, and updated linens would be needed across the board. I did find it odd that there was a lack of dust, considering they had clearly not been in use recently.

"Val," Leo explained. "She's the housekeeper. She comes every Friday. She does a grocery pickup and tidies around the house." I sensed there was more to it, but I didn't press him.

However, Val remained elusive, as Leo requested we leave her to her work on the first two Fridays, and instead we headed out to a handful of local businesses I had scouted to take a look at—tile, countertops, fixtures, and fittings.

Shopping with Leo became a fun escape. He insisted on driving, and owned a brand-new and exquisite luxury sports car. I marveled at the soft leather seats and enjoyed relaxing next to him while he drove through the countryside. My pleasure at his car seemed to amuse him.

While we drove along the country roads, with the crisp fall air biting through the open sunroof, I often found myself observing Leo. He was so much more carefree outside of the house, especially on those long drives. It became more difficult not to notice the mounting number of differences between Leo and Adam, much to my dismay.

Things remained stagnant in my relationship, and while

I would never dream of cheating on a partner, it didn't escape my notice that my thoughts kept drifting to what being in a relationship with Leo would be like. The more I got to know him, the more he opened up to me, the more information I craved.

I hadn't ever felt that hunger for knowledge with Adam. He had always been so transparent to me, despite his best efforts to hide behind his well-manicured appearance and tailored suits. But so much of Leo remained an enigma, luring me into what was surely a trap within the stuffy confines of Willowbrooke.

"What's our first stop again?" Leo asked, bringing me crashing out of my reverie.

"Tileworks," I replied absently.

"Excellent." He flashed me what had once been a rare grin but was slowly becoming much more common in these quiet moments between the two of us.

I worried at first that Leo might become bored with sourcing all the materials and making so many small decisions, but he never once complained or acted in a way that made me think he was annoyed with the process. While he typically defaulted to me on decisions, he spoke up if he felt strongly about something, and true to his word, money seemed to be of no object.

Throughout the first few weeks, outside those brief flashes of candor on our road trips, Leo remained aloof and reserved, but occasionally I would get glimpses of him letting his guard down, like when he'd reassure himself quietly, "Dad would like that," or something similar, after picking a specific component.

I was sympathetic to his grief, as he was so deeply impacted by the loss of his father, and I wondered what he had been like before. Had he always been so solemn and solitary? I was desperate to know more, and I did sense the very early seeds of a potential friendship blooming between the two of us.

Did he feel the same?

Could you be friends with someone who never shared a single thing about themself with you?

Could I be satisfied with such a mysterious acquaintance?

The answer to all of the above was *probably not.*

I was beginning to enjoy the routine Leo and I had started to settle into. He'd have a fresh, hot cup of coffee waiting for me every morning at eight a.m. on the dot. We'd review our plan for the day over said coffee, and get to work.

At first I brought lunch with me, but after a couple of days, Leo started ordering in for us, which was a nice treat and one less thing for me to worry about, considering how the long commute and continued distance from Adam was weighing on me.

Leo's small, kind gestures further exacerbated the conflicting feelings escalating inside of me over my relationship with Adam. Leo was my boss, and that was a line

I couldn't cross…a line I shouldn't even be thinking about in the first place.

But being appreciated and considered by someone made me realize maybe I didn't want things to work out with Adam. I didn't think he was capable of treating me how I wanted to be treated.

The thought of ending things made my stomach knot up. Confrontation had never been a strength of mine, and Adam always had a way of twisting what I was saying and thinking to make me feel he was in the right.

"Dare I ask how things are going with Adam?" Mina asked delicately over coffee one weekend.

"I don't know…" I hedged.

"Penny." Mina's tone took on a warning note.

"He's been working closely with a new architect at the firm, lots of late nights on the project." I sighed. "I've just been a little lonely, is all."

"New *female* architect?" she asked hesitantly.

"Yeah…"

I had never been the jealous type before meeting Adam two years ago, since I had known going in that he was a flirt. It was just the kind of guy he was. In the beginning, things were so intense that it took a while for me to realize that kind of behavior, no matter how innocent, made me feel insecure.

It was quite the whirlwind romance after he'd started at the firm. We'd moved in together quickly, and he'd swiftly risen up the ranks at my parents' architecture firm.

Any time I mentioned my discomfort with him being overly friendly with the female staff, he'd explain the situation, which always sounded so much more reasonable when it came from him, and then I'd be left feeling silly for being jealous, wondering if it was all in my head.

Our relationship as of late had become a bit more tenuous. I'd get upset over feeling neglected, and he'd be mad that I hadn't given him the benefit of the doubt. It was a never-ending, vicious cycle that I hadn't found a way to exit. I'd never struggled in a relationship the way I did with Adam.

Before I'd met Leo and realized the disparity in how Adam treated me compared to the way Leo did, there had been moments of love and clarity that I'd clung to, that had made me want to fight to be with him. Those moments seemed to pale in comparison to the possibilities I saw on the horizon, in a future without Adam.

Between my recent realizations and Mina's validation, I was left spiraling, wondering if all this time and effort spent trying to make things work was even worth it.

I already knew the answer. The question was if I was ready to do anything about it.

"Are you going to talk to him?" she asked softly.

Having been on the other side, trying to pull Mina out of an emotionally abusive relationship in college, I knew she was wary of alienating me. It could backfire and push me toward him, rather than pulling me away. She was trying to be supportive, while making sure I knew her stance on the matter.

"And tell him what?" I slumped in my seat. "I already know what he's going to say, that he's just friends with Zoe, and that I need to trust him."

Mina leaned forward, reaching for my hand across the table. "Penny, you know you could stay with me."

"I know." I nodded. "I'm not there yet."

"What's really holding you back?" she asked.

I met her gaze. "When I talk to him about how I'm feeling, he explains things in a way that makes sense in the moment, but then later, it just makes me more confused." I wasn't quite sure how to vocalize how mixed up I felt about everything.

"Adam always seems to have an answer to everything," Mina observed.

"He's always so eager to make things work, and tries to find a solution to make things better, but then lets everything fall apart again." I blinked back tears.

I knew the writing was on the wall. I knew what advice I would give Mina if she was in the same situation, but every time I got up the courage to try to confront Adam about my misgivings, he just had this way to make them all disappear.

"Like the day I gave my two weeks' at the firm," I brought up as an example. "After we talked through why I didn't tell him about it before, he offered to take me to dinner to celebrate my new job. But we never went."

"What?"

"He ended up having to work late at the office on his big project and forgot about it." I felt a twinge of embarrassment, even though it had happened weeks prior.

"What do you mean he 'forgot'?" Mina gritted her teeth.

"I mean, I got dressed up and sat at the apartment, waiting for him to get home, and fell asleep on the couch. But he brought me flowers the next day to make up for it," I added, knowing it wasn't enough. "I thought maybe he'd try to take me out a different night, but he never brought it up again after the flowers."

"He's always been all talk." Mina couldn't hold back any longer. "But you didn't answer my question. What will it take for you to leave, Penny?"

"Courage." I frowned.

Leo and Willowbrooke brought much-needed distraction into my life while I struggled to figure out how and when to end things with Adam.

While Leo and I were slowly warming up to each other, the house was a different story altogether.

Despite the constant natural light I insisted upon, the atmosphere remained heavy. I felt safer with Leo's comforting presence nearby, but when alone, I was easily spooked by noises and tricks of the light that had me questioning my sanity. I always made sure to leave before dark, an increasingly difficult task as fall progressed, not to mention the guilt it instilled as I worried that I was leaving Leo with a bad impression of my work ethic.

I tried to brush off the weird feeling, the tingling at the back of my neck when I was alone in a room, or the sense of being watched. But one day, a few weeks into the project, I couldn't ignore my instincts any longer.

While doing the furniture inventory, I had used my phone to take as professional "before" shots of the home as I could. I was referencing one of the photos of the pink room, one of the three guest bedrooms upstairs, when I noticed an odd shadow in the corner, but it was absent from the subsequent photos. On top of that, there were weird light specks littered across the last few photos of the same room.

"Leo, come look at this." I beckoned him from the storage room behind the kitchen, where he was sorting through a wall of junk that had accumulated—our project now also seemed to include both organizing and decluttering the entire house, but I didn't mind, because it meant more time with Leo.

Leo sauntered out of the room and glanced at my camera, but he just shrugged, unimpressed with the photos.

"That's not normal," I declared, swiping back and forth between the photo with the shadow and the next one, the same composition, where it was gone. "And what about the specks?"

"It's just dust, Penny," he dismissed me, already on his way back to the storage room.

"That shadow isn't dust!" I called after him. I created a new folder on my laptop and decided to throw any incriminating photos into it. Maybe if I had more evidence, he'd believe me. Not that there was anything either of us could do about it, if the house was haunted, but I would have appreciated some validation.

A week later, another incident transpired in the basement. Leo remembered there might be extra dining chairs and a table leaf down there, and asked if I could check it out.

The basement was a whole other level of terrifying.

Only lit by two dangling and dim light bulbs hanging on opposite ends of the expansive space, the basement had never been touched by any of the previous renovations. Save for a new set of stairs descending into the must and cobwebs, it looked as it would have when the house was built in the eighteen hundreds.

"You want me to go down there alone!?" I croaked.

Leo raised a brow, biting back his amusement at my terror, and challenging me to refuse.

I gulped, nervous, but still determined to stay in his good graces, and made my way down to the basement, using my phone as a flashlight as I tried to locate the missing furniture. Sound was oddly muffled, perhaps by the stone walls. It felt as though I was in a different house entirely.

I thought I heard a scraping behind me, but when I spun my phone around, nobody was there. I was becoming desperate to find the stupid chairs and debated going back up and admitting defeat, when something touched my shoulder.

I let out a bloodcurdling scream, only to be met by laughter…Leo's laughter.

"Oh, Penny," he wheezed, placing a hand around my shoulder, pulling me into his side, in apology, "I'm so sorry." He held his other hand over his chest, trying to slow his breathing. "I didn't mean to scare you."

"What the hell, Leo!?" I pushed him away.

"I came down to help you look," he sighed, still trying to get over his amusement at just how badly he had frightened me. "I'm sorry, Pen."

But then a strange thing happened…I started laughing too. I saw how silly I was being, but it also dawned on me that it was the first time I'd heard Leo laugh, and the sound was simply glorious.

CHAPTER 3

MARGOT

The inspector recommendations Mina made came in clutch, as Joe Mortimer, the inspector Leo ended up hiring, seemed to have been an old friend of his Uncle William, another specter in Leo's life I had yet to meet. William came up every now and again in conversation, along with Val the housekeeper, Carl the gardener, and his infamous Aunt Margot. Leo's adoration for his aunt was hard for even his somewhat unreadable demeanor to hide. But none of these people had materialized in the house, despite my growing desperation to gain more insight into the puzzle that was Leo West.

Inspector Joe was as seasoned as he was salty and left no

stone unturned or truth untold. While Leo winced at the prospect of having to redo the roof in the next five years, there were a few windows that needed to be replaced in the library, and Joe suggested he could make a return visit once the kitchen had been gutted, if the contractors had any concerns above their abilities. He also mentioned that we should be careful in the basement, but didn't elaborate, at least not while I was around. Leo was unfazed by the comment.

Joe left with a spate of compliments about how well the house had been maintained for its age and a promise from Leo to say 'hi' to his Uncle William on Joe's behalf.

The plan for the space was quite ambitious, but I felt it was well within my means. The kitchen would be the first and the largest job, with almost full demolition, new cabinetry, new countertops, new flooring, and new appliances. Leo had agreed with me to put a fresh coat of paint on and pull up the carpeting across the entire home with the intention of refinishing the original hardwood floors beneath.

The bathrooms would also require new cabinetry, tiling, and fixtures. If the bathrooms had any original features left, I would have tried to keep them, but the renovation in the eighties had taken out anything worth preserving. The one good thing was that I didn't plan on doing any major reconfigurations. Otherwise, it was all down to details, like hardware, lighting options, soft finishings, replacing every single dust-laden curtain in the place, and my favorite part, the styling.

If only our other contractors had been as easy as Joe the inspector.

Leo and I spent a week interviewing the entire list of people Mina had given me to lead the actual construction that would be required for the house.

He wasn't impressed with any of them.

While Leo remained impassive and polite during the interviews, after each was dismissed, he would provide me with a vague determination of why it wouldn't work out: too inexperienced, too busy, not enough connections with specialty contractors, the list went on. The final straw came when our last potential lead contractor and Mina's highest recommendation somehow agitated Leo, resulting in him ending the interview early and asking the contractor to leave.

"What was that about?" I sighed in exasperation, after escorting the contractor outside.

Leo's jaw clenched as he poured himself a glass of red wine, something he frequently did toward the end of the day, although he usually waited until I was on my way out the door to break out his first glass.

"Well?" I wasn't going to let him get away that easily. Hands on hips, I blocked his path out of the kitchen.

"I don't care to employ misogynists," he said simply, circumventing me to make his way to the living room.

"What?" I replied, completely confused, and followed right behind him. "What are you talking about, Leo?"

Gracefully, Leo reclined on the new sectional, which

had arrived only the day before, crossing one ankle over the opposite knee, swirling the wine in his glass, but careful not to let a drop spill. "The lot of them spoke singularly to me." He raised his eyes from his glass to meet my gaze.

"You're the client," I replied, still not understanding how he saw them as sexist.

"But *you're* the project manager," he countered before taking a sip of his wine. "You scheduled the meetings, you greeted them, you explained the plans, our needs for the project, and answered every single technical question they had. It couldn't have been more obvious that you're the lead on this, and yet, not a single one of them spoke to you—the last didn't even make eye contact."

I could feel my brow furrow as I recalled all the interviews, running through each one, trying to identify any relevant exchange that had been made between me and the various men we had interviewed. "I hadn't noticed..." I trailed off, realizing he was correct.

I sat down next to him on the couch. "I think I'm so used to people just ignoring me at the firm—it didn't occur to me that they should have addressed me." I looked down at my shoes. I'd need a new pair of white sneakers in the next couple months, the rubber on the sole was wearing thin. "I'm sorry," I mumbled.

"Oh no." Leo shook his head. "Don't start apologizing."

I looked up at him, confused.

"*You* didn't do anything wrong—*you* have nothing to

apologize for. You're learning. They're grown men who can't wrap their heads around a woman being in charge." He took another sip of wine.

I hadn't seen him so wound up before.

"You could have just corrected them," I offered, my voice feeling smaller than ever.

"Penny." Leo's tone commanded my eye contact, which I obliged. "You don't want to work with someone who doesn't immediately provide their respect. We need to find someone who understands you're in control, without having to be told." He gave a slight nod of his head, as if to confirm my understanding.

"Thank you." I offered a curt smile. It had been a long time since someone had stood up for me like that, other than Mina. I tried to ignore the now familiar but unwanted flutter in my stomach.

"My uncle said he'd send over a friend next week that would be a good fit—friends with the inspector, it seems— so I'm sure he'll be alright." Leo leaned back into the couch, swirling his glass again.

"It's getting dark outside," I replied, rising from my seat next to him. "I better get going." I felt awkward and out of sorts as I made my way to the front door. I was preoccupied, shuffling through memories of my experiences with the interviews and how I had so grossly misperceived each contractor's intentions and communication, or rather, lack thereof.

On top of that, seeing Leo reclined so casually felt too intimate. He was my boss. It was bad enough that I had started to harbor a small crush, just because he treated me with respect, but even worse that I was still trying to figure out how to get out of my relationship with Adam.

"Drive safe, Penny." Leo raised his wineglass to me, and I responded with a small wave before leaving the house for my car, hoping he hadn't seen the flush on my cheeks.

Even though so much of Leo was closed off to me, small exchanges like what I had just experienced offered a wealth of nuanced character study.

Leo was loyal.

He was willing to fight for me, protect me, when I had done nothing to earn it from him.

Maybe we could become friends after all…

Just friends, I had to remind myself.

William's hunch on the construction foreman was a good one. Just as grizzled as Inspector Joe, Danny Bright seemed to have connections to everyone, and his gregarious nature was surely the reason why.

Leo immediately took to Danny, and Danny seemed just as fond of me, which pleased Leo. Danny would often go into tutorials, teaching me (and Leo, if he was around), about whatever project he or one of his guys was working on. His lessons were usually quite long-winded, but nothing if not informative, and I appreciated learning more about the intricacies of various construction processes.

If Danny disagreed with one of my design decisions based on the methods he was using or due to his decades of experience building and renovating homes, we would talk through the importance of my decision, or how we might compromise to both get what we wanted out of the change.

And Danny was fast too.

Demolition of the kitchen took a little over a day. His team was able to salvage a good chunk of the materials, which were donated to a local nonprofit, and they carefully relocated the refrigerator to the dining room, while we waited for the new integrated and panel-ready one to be delivered in less than two weeks.

Leo seemed antsy at the prospect of losing full access to the kitchen for two weeks, but I believed the thought of having a brand new, bespoke space that was customized to his needs and not falling apart at the seams would be well worth the wait and a couple weeks of takeout.

Toward the end of the first week with Danny, he and I found ourselves arguing about the style of sink I was getting ready to purchase. He felt the counter slab that Leo and I had chosen from the stone yard was beautiful enough that it warranted a seamless sink, where the counter material was used to form the sink, rather than purchasing one separately.

Having looked up some quick example photos on my phone, I liked the idea, and we had just begun talking through what kind of hardware I was going to need to order for the drain, when a gasp from the front door stopped our conversation in its tracks.

In the doorframe stood a woman who was slight *only* in stature, as everything else about her, from her three-inch stilettos, to her impeccably tailored designer coat, down to her pointed crimson fingernails, commanded the room.

"What happened to the kitchen?" Her voice was silken, with a trace of an unidentifiable accent that could have been from her world travels, or an intentional affectation to make sure people knew she was well traveled. Her alarmed eyes bounced back and forth between Danny and I, no doubt wondering who we were, as much as the both of us were clueless to her identity.

"Aunt Margot!" Leo called out as he rounded the hallway leading to his room and the solarium, having heard the commotion.

So she was the much lauded Aunt Margot.

She wasn't at all as I had expected.

Based on Leo's loving description of her, I had expected a woman who embodied motherhood and coziness, but this woman was, much like Leo, something else entirely, and another knot to unravel.

"Leo, darling!" she cooed, leaving a bright red lipstick stain on his cheek before they embraced tightly.

"I thought you were staying at the chateau for another few weeks." Leo stepped back, as if to take all of her in. I had never seen him more open and engaged. I wondered if this was what Leo had been like before his father had passed away…before he had taken the weight of the world, and of Willowbrooke, on his shoulders.

"The routine became tiresome, and I missed you, so I came back early," she explained before looking around and remarking, "Dear nephew, what on earth have you done to my house?"

"It's what Dad wanted," Leo said quietly, his expression and body language making him look like a child seeking approval, rather than the strong but stoic man I had found him to be in our time together.

Margot sighed sympathetically. "Of course." She patted his cheek gently, accepting his explanation. "Well, don't be rude, introduce me to your guests." Margot turned her sharp hazel eyes—the same as Leo's—on Danny and me.

"Penny Abbot, my interior designer and project manager." He motioned to me first.

"Margot Collins, a pleasure." Margot stuck her hand out to shake mine in a soft exchange.

"Leo's told me all about you." I looked beyond Margot to meet Leo's gaze. I might have imagined it, but I thought it appeared as though his cheeks flushed for a brief moment. "It's nice to finally put a face to a name."

Margot turned around to look at Leo. "Now what kind of stories have you been sharing?" she teased. "Only good things, I hope."

Leo quirked a smile, but didn't respond.

Margot shifted back to me. "I'm surprised you've gotten anything out of him." She smiled mischievously through her eyelash extensions. "Leo's never been exactly forthcoming about much."

Leo sighed at the jab, which made Margot giggle.

"And who might this handsome young man be?" She sidestepped me to shake hands with Danny, who wasn't at all fazed by her intended compliment, as he was easily in his sixties.

"Danny Bright—construction foreman." He gave an uneasy smile and returned the handshake. "Nice to meet you, ma'am." I was surprised Danny, who usually had oodles to say, was suddenly quiet. I resolved to ask him about it later. Perhaps he had met her before, since he was so well entrenched in the area.

"Now then, Leo. Can someone take my bags to the cottage?" Margot returned to Leo's side. "I thought we'd catch up over a glass of wine, but we'll have to pop the cork over at mine to stay out of this mess." She waved her hand at Danny and I, standing in the deconstructed kitchen.

"I've got it," Leo told Margot, simultaneously notifying Danny and me to stand down.

And without another word, the two were out the door.

"Cat got your tongue?" I gave Danny a playful shove.

"I find it best to stay quiet around people of a certain class," he replied gruffly, which was uncharacteristic of him.

I thought it odd that he didn't seem to consider Leo of the same class as Margot; if anything, Leo's inheritance would have made him much more well off than his aunt.

Not wanting to push him further, I let the subject drop. "So the fittings—do you think they'll come in aged brass? That's what Leo wanted for all the kitchen fixtures."

"I know a guy," Danny offered, a response that was so common, it could have been his catchphrase.

"I bet you do," I laughed.

A few days later, Margot found me examining sheer curtain samples in the living room. I was excited to surprise Leo with the double curtains, so without sacrificing the light, he could keep the sheer curtains drawn, which seemed to be his preference, although he humored me by allowing them to stay open while I was at the house.

"I'm taking you to lunch, Miss Abbot," she declared, wearing a conservative navy blue shift dress, and another pair of sky-high heels with a red sole that I merely recognized as expensive.

"Oh, I couldn't—I've got to submit the drapery order today," I tried. "But thank you so much for the offer."

"Nonsense—I already told Leo—he doesn't mind." Margot's red lips curled at her victory.

I paused for a moment, but realized I had been defeated. "Alright." I gave a polite smile as I rose from my seat.

"Excellent!" She looped her arm through mine and led me out to her car, which was just as glossy and crimson as her nails.

Before I could even ask where we were off to, Margot began talking a mile a minute, asking all sorts of questions.

"Leo tells me your family is in architecture—why didn't you follow in the trade?" She expertly handled a steep curve as she spoke.

"I tried," I admitted, "but design was my passion." I tried to focus on the positive, rather than my failures.

"A new passion, though?" Margot corrected me. "Leo said this is your first project of this size."

"Not a new passion." I paused, trying to work through exactly how to give her information without making myself sound less than—both Mina and now sometimes Leo had been after me to work on my self-confidence.

"When I graduated, my parents needed help at their firm, so I worked there for a while, but eventually—I just…" I stumbled over my words. "I wanted to find my own career— my own path."

"A risky gamble," Margot commented, her eyes firmly on the road ahead of her. "Quite admirable."

"Thank you." I blushed at the compliment.

I found Margot intimidating, but because Leo cared for her so deeply, I couldn't deny wanting to impress her. I felt it was important that she think highly of me—maybe I was scared that if she didn't like me, Leo would change his mind, and all of the good fortune I had stumbled upon would be lost.

"Tell me, what are your honest thoughts about Willowbrooke?" she simpered.

I couldn't help but smile at the thought of the home, haunted or not. "I love it," I said simply.

Margot nodded in response, but said nothing more as she pulled into the driveway of an ivy-covered building that housed the restaurant. She waited for the valet to open her car door, whereas I didn't have the manners or experience to realize I should have followed her lead and done the same.

"Do they have a dress code here?" I tugged at my oversized blazer and pursed my lips, trying not to look down at my sneakers, which were covered in dust from the kitchen construction.

"Probably," she said flippantly. "But the owner is a dear friend—so nobody will give you any trouble."

I had to smother a grimace when we crossed the threshold to a sea of blue bloods dressed in their finest, as Margot had clearly taken me to a fancy dining establishment.

"Pierre!" Margot gushed, giving air kisses to an attractive older man wearing an immaculate black suit and a thin mustache. With the way he carried himself, he had to be the owner she'd spoken of.

"How was Europe?" Pierre beamed.

"Oh you know, nice for a while, but there's no place like home," Margot chatted. "I hope you kept my table open for me."

"But of course, right this way." He allowed her to politely rest her hand on his arm as he escorted her to the back of the dining room. I followed like a dope, as the man had never even made notice of me.

"Madam." He smiled, pulling out Margot's chair for her. Once again, I committed a faux pas by seating myself. I didn't think I'd ever been to such an expensive restaurant before. I hoped Margot wouldn't count it against me.

"Shall I bring over your usual?" Pierre asked Margot.

"That would be lovely." She smiled up at the gentleman. "And she'll have the same."

Pierre nodded without a glance in my direction before he was off.

"Bit of a social climber, but an excellent contact to have nonetheless." Margot neatly folded her cloth napkin over her lap.

I laughed at the remark because I got the impression that was the response she had wanted. And indeed, she smiled in acknowledgement.

"In the car—you didn't tell me, what do *you* think of Willowbrooke?" I tried to start polite conversation.

Before she could answer, a waiter brought us both glasses of red wine.

Margot sighed appreciatively, "Chateau Gardelier, Cabernet, 1978 vintage." She swirled her wineglass. "It's where I was staying in Europe—one of my friends owns it. Stunning vineyards and gardens. You'll have to visit sometime."

I found the offer hollow, but nodded politely anyway.

Following her lead, I also gently swirled my glass. I enjoyed a glass of red every now and again, but was far from an expert in anything having to do with wine. Leo likely would have been appalled to know I had a box of red sitting in my apartment as I dined with his aunt.

I took a small sip—it wasn't as dry as I had expected. "It's good," I said genuinely, eyebrows raised in delight.

Margot seemed pleased and inhaled the scent of her glass before drinking from it. "It's odd staying at the cottage now— since the divorce a few years ago. We were never allowed to go near the cottage growing up, as the groundskeeper lived there at the time. You'll have to come by and visit, give me your advice on the design. It's a bit too homey for my liking. I prefer residences that are more stately.

"Willowbrooke is a complicated place for me—for my family." She circled back to my question. "I grew up there—I have a lot of happy memories in the house." She paused before taking another sip of her wine, "But the house has also seen a lot of tragedy, which can be difficult to ignore."

I remained quiet, interested in what little information Margot was willing to share with me, as Leo had said nothing of it.

"The air in the house gets quite heavy—sometimes I think it's the spirits of those who passed on the grounds," she said solemnly.

"Spirits—plural?" I asked faintly, picturing the odd shadow and orbs in the photos I had taken, sending a shiver down my spine.

Margot sighed. "Well—those that I know of—my father and mother, Leo's mother, Christine—and now George, my brother. I'm sure there were more before, since our family built the house."

I opened my mouth to ask what I really wanted to know, but paused. I knew I shouldn't, but I couldn't help myself. "How?" I whispered.

Margot's gaze met mine, and although I expected malice or at least discomfort, she was instead curious. "Daddy had a bad heart—back then it was hard to know in advance—I found him in the study. Mother was devastated and died of a broken heart not long after." She looked beyond me, as if she was peering into the memory.

She took a long sip of the wine. "Christine—poor thing, I think she found motherhood difficult, as they don't warn you about anything, how it changes you, how it's not meant for everyone—it certainly wasn't meant for me." Margot raised her glass, "She couldn't cope—decided to end things on her own terms…"

Was Margot implying Leo's mother had committed suicide?

"Such awful business, and George never got over it, never got over her. It changed him."

We sat for a moment, the air heavy between us.

"And what of George?" I said softly, entranced by Margot's transparency.

"Cancer. But George didn't like going to the doctor, so they didn't have a chance to do much treatment—it all happened so quickly." Margot's eyes were glassy, thinking of her brother, who might have sat in this very chair across from her mere months prior.

"I'm sorry," I whispered. I wanted to reach across the table and comfort her, but thought better of it.

"I'm just glad he reconciled with Leo before the end." She sniffled. "George spent years pushing that poor little boy away—reminded him too much of Christine, I think. Poor thing's an orphan at thirty-five—still too young."

"But he still has you," I offered sympathetically.

Margot gave me a watery smile. "And now you, it seems."

"Me?" I was taken aback by her inference.

"He's quite fond of you, you know?" She raised an eyebrow, gauging my response to the revelation.

"I'm fond of him." I softened. "He makes for an excellent client." I chose my words deliberately to make sure she understood the extent of our relationship.

"And what exactly makes an excellent client? Deep pockets and a handsome face?" Margot laughed.

I was shocked at the implication, but decided to give her the benefit of the doubt. "The fact that he actually trusts my opinion and doesn't argue over small details." I smiled. "I'm very lucky to have this project." My tone sobered.

"Yes," she agreed. "Yes, you are."

Again, I wasn't sure if I was reading Margot correctly. Was I imagining the edge to her voice, the hint of a threat behind her words?

"He's lucky to have you; I think you've really helped him through his grieving process—he's never had many friends, you know." Margot's tone was even now…sincere. Maybe she just had a quirky sense of humor.

"He's easy to get along with," I said honestly, not revealing that it was only true because he rarely revealed much of himself. You couldn't argue or have trouble with someone you barely knew. And you certainly shouldn't be harboring crushes on them either, especially when you worked for them.

"I wonder if you would have liked him as much before— he was a bit of a shark in his career. Recent events have softened him, for the better, I think."

"What did he do before?"

Mina and I had often speculated, and even found some vague news articles that mentioned his name, but nothing concrete. And I was too nervous to ask Leo, if he didn't want to offer it up first.

"Leo's brilliant—a self-made entrepreneur. He built a great reputation for himself, helping start-ups scale their businesses and secure funding for expansions." Margot smiled as she spoke. "And look at you, starting your own business. Birds of a feather, I suppose."

I scoffed. "I don't have a business."

"Not yet," Margot tutted.

"I wouldn't know where to start. The business side of things are quite a bit out of my skill set." I hadn't meant to let my insecurity show, but it seemed being honest with Margot was more important than pretending.

"You should ask Leo for help. He figured it all out on his own. He never took a dime from George—not that George would have given him a thing back then. They had a falling out shortly after Leo graduated high school, and they both went their own ways. It broke my heart to see them so distant, but I think even then I knew they both required time apart to see that they needed each other." Margot finished her glass of wine.

"George was so proud of his boy—Leo's an only child, after all. But damned if he couldn't actually communicate those words with Leo. It took a long time, and a lot of cajoling on my end to get Leo to come back and make amends before it was too late. But thank god he did." Margot raised her hand at a passing waitress and pointed to her empty glass. The girl nodded and hurried to the bar for a refill.

I wondered if Leo's lack of approval from his father was one of the reasons that we got along so well. We understood what it was like to deal with conditional love from a parent, when what you so desperately desired was simply acceptance. I could relate to what Leo had gone through with his family, although certainly to a lesser degree.

"Leo dropped everything, gave up his old life, his career, his business, everything he built, and moved back home to take care of his father. They talked about renovating the house when George got better—but they both knew Leo alone would take up the mantle. It was George's last wish to revive the house, to restore it to its former glory and move past the tragedies that occurred there, for a fresh start—for Leo. And you are giving that to him—you are helping his vision of restoration come to life. You are providing a new beginning." Margot smiled sadly.

"It's my pleasure," I offered. Her words mirrored Leo's so perfectly. It seemed both Leo and Margot were ready to move forward and start anew.

"I worry Leo's still in denial about the whole thing—it's only been a few months. Even I forget sometimes. I half expected George to be the one to greet me when I arrived home the other day. And poor Leo—he won't even step foot in the solarium." She shook her head.

"What happened in there?" I asked, biting my cheek to hide my nerves, but still failing miserably.

"Leo didn't tell you?" she asked, flashing a swift smile at the waitress as she set down a fresh glass of wine.

"No." I shook my head.

"It's where George died," she said matter-of-factly before taking a drink of her wine.

CHAPTER 4

SOLARIUM

A couple days later, after another awkward weekend of walking on eggshells with Adam at the apartment, I was still shaken by everything Margot had divulged. I was glad to have so much more insight into Leo, but I felt guilty that none of the information had come directly from him.

I was surprised Margot had been so open with me. Maybe she thought it would be better for Leo if I knew. That way, he didn't have to talk about all the things he clearly preferred to leave in the past.

How would he feel if he knew Margot had been so open about his history? If I found out Leo went to my parents or my sister, Sloan, to learn more about me, I would definitely be upset…but if they'd gone to him…it wouldn't be as cut and dry.

Still, my discussion with Margot weighed heavily on me.

Leo was out for lunch with his Uncle William, who Margot informed me was not in fact Leo's actual uncle, but rather his father's old business partner. Margot also confided that she suspected he was the angel investor who had helped Leo get his own consulting business off the ground.

My introduction to William Mitchell was brief.

With broad shoulders, a square jaw, and a full head of salt-and-pepper hair, he looked the part of a wealthy businessman and investor. To me, every bit of him screamed old money. But he was just as polite as he was well-dressed, and apologized for the hurried meeting as Leo practically pushed him out the door, saying they'd miss their lunch reservation if they didn't leave right away.

I wondered what Leo was so worried about. Would William be as loose-lipped as his aunt? After all, if Leo and William were as close as Margot made it seem, William would have even more insight into Leo's recent history, as Margot and her nephew had only reconnected when she'd reached out asking him to make amends with his father. More than a decade of Leo's life had been lost to Margot, but William had been there every step of the way.

But then, I thought about what Danny had said after meeting Margot, that he was wary of people of a certain class.

Was Leo afraid of what impression William would make on me? Or perhaps he didn't want William to have too much time to assess me? I suppose I'd never know—for the most part, Leo was still a closed book.

Rather than dwell on the clumsy interaction, I made myself busy checking things off my ever-growing to-do list. I had just come down the back stairs after taking some measurements for the upcoming flooring contractors when I spotted something amiss.

At first, I could only deduce that there was something off on the main floor. Then I realized it was the lighting that was brighter.

And it was brighter because the door to the solarium at the far end of the house was wide open…

The house in which I was supposed to be completely alone.

"Leo?" I called out. I waited a minute for a response, but heard nothing.

"Hello?" I tried once more.

Nothing.

I audibly gulped, before slowly making my way across the home, walking toward the north hallway, which was off-limits, per Leo's strict instructions—his *one* rule.

At first I told myself that I would just close the door, but like a moth to a flame, and without anyone else around, I found myself passing through the threshold, my stomach sinking as I broke the invisible barrier to the previously forbidden room.

I reasoned that I probably should check the room for drafts, or the door for damage, to fix whatever had caused it to unlatch itself. The mission made me feel better about entering the room, but the twist in the pit of my stomach telling me that it was wrong to be in there refused to subside. The room's atmosphere made me want to run far from Willowbrooke.

Like the turreted master above the solarium, the room was almost a complete circle, with straight edges only near the entrance, where the room adjoined the rest of the house and connected to a jack and jill bathroom that passed through to Leo's bedroom. The hardwood floors, in the same herringbone pattern I had discovered across the rest of the house, were on full display. I wondered why this was the only place in the entire house that had been spared from the 80's carpet installation.

Immediately upon entering, I was hit with the standard sterile and antiseptic smell that immediately transports anyone who has been to a hospital spiraling back into some trauma that took place within the walls of a medical facility. For me, it was the memory of my grandmother dying when I was ten.

My parents had ushered me and Sloan into the room where she was drawing her last breaths, a husk of herself from the few memories I had of her from an earlier age. She was already in an induced coma, and we were instructed to say our goodbyes, assured by Mom and Dad that she could hear us, even though she looked like she was sleeping.

I hadn't managed any words through my tears, not understanding exactly what had happened to her, but knowing just enough to realize I wouldn't see her again after we left the room.

Sloan, ever the perfect daughter and half automaton, had told Grandma how much she loved her and that she would miss her, but that they would see each other again in heaven. She thanked her for always taking us out to ice cream, even though Mom told her not to. My mother frowned at this discovery. I was pleased with her discomfort, but mad at Sloan for betraying Grandma's trust.

I guess a twelve-year-old Sloan understood that the secret no longer mattered. Then she told Grandma it was okay for her to go, that we'd be okay, and that she knew Grandma would always watch over us.

Sloan's words had sent me into another fit of sobs, which seemed to annoy my parents, as they profusely apologized to the nurses that stared or whispered while we made our way back to the car.

I have hated hospitals ever since.

It was one of the first times I remember feeling so alone and understanding how much of a disappointment I was to my parents.

I took a deep breath, shaking off the melancholy.

The solarium was sparse save for a wingback chair and

George West's expensive medical bed. The sheets were neatly and tightly tucked into the mattress, which was angled to help him sit up. A table on wheels was next to the bed, opposite the wingback chair, with a half complete crossword puzzle and pencil sitting precisely where George, or maybe Leo, had left it the day George died.

Everything seemed to be exactly as it had been before he passed. Curiously, there was a fine layer of dust over everything in the room, which meant that even Val wasn't allowed to enter.

I caught the dust swirling in the afternoon sunlight streaming through the windows—the uncovered windows.

It hit me then that all of the curtains were open, which was why the light had attracted my attention from the opposite end of the house. But I knew for a fact Leo always kept them drawn, because every morning when I pulled up and every night when I left, they were closed—not letting a ray of light or a prying eye anywhere near the space.

Feeling exposed, and suddenly remembering the excuse I had given myself for entering the room, I began to go around closing the curtains, panel by panel. I had made it halfway around the room when I heard a noise coming from the hallway.

I turned to find Leo in the doorway, eyes ablaze, and William behind him, looking stunned. "What the FUCK, Penny?" Leo seethed.

Without warning, a flood of words and excuses spewed

from me as I tried desperately to explain why I had disobeyed Leo and trespassed into the one room he had asked me not to enter. "I came downstairs and the door was open. Someone opened all the curtains. I was just trying to put everything back the way it was—"

Leo put his hand up, stopping me mid-sentence.

I immediately obeyed.

His eyes met mine—he was furious. "Get. Out," he said slowly and deliberately.

"Leo, I'm sorry, I didn't open the door—I know I'm not supposed to come in here—I was trying to help—" I tried in vain to make him understand.

"Get! Out!" he thundered, furious eyes still fixed on mine, silencing me.

I could hear my pulse pounding in my ears. I glanced between Leo and William. The latter looked helpless and confused. He wouldn't come to my rescue and talk sense into Leo on my behalf. Why would he? He didn't even know me.

Holding my breath, I made a beeline past the two men, unable to look at either of them. I could feel my face burning and tears pricking at my eyes. What had I done?

I cried the entire drive back to the apartment as I tried to mentally compose an apology that would somehow salvage my dream project and my relationship with Leo.

It dawned on me through tears that despite the growing anxiety over my decomposing relationship with Adam, I had never been happier with my career. I looked forward to seeing

Leo and working on the house every day.

In a short two months, I had felt my confidence grow; I had thought I was forming a real friendship with Leo, and I was finding my groove. But now all of that was gone—in the blink of an eye.

Leo hadn't even given me a chance to explain.

He had to know I would never go into the solarium without his permission unless I felt it was necessary. But that place—what had happened there...reason didn't seem to matter to him when it came to the solarium or his father. And Leo didn't strike me as the kind of person to easily forgive and forget. How could he welcome me back into his home after I'd violated him?

In an effort to protect myself, I turned my phone off. I was already operating under the assumption that all was lost, so when I inevitably got the call or email saying my services were no longer needed, I could face the consequences of my actions as prepared as one could be for that kind of communication, rather than allowing myself to be caught off guard.

I was wracked with guilt and an overwhelming sense of doom. What was I going to do? How was I supposed to explain any of this to anyone? I didn't want to bother Mina, as she was out of the country, traveling with a new boyfriend.

I had no one.

Even though I'd left Willowbrooke early, traffic was backed up due to an accident, and it was well after dark when I finally made it back to my apartment in the city.

My day was about to go from bad to worse.

"Miss Abbot! Miss Abbot!" the doorman called after me as I trudged through the lobby.

He stopped in his tracks when I turned to regard him and saw my red, puffy, tearstained face. I said nothing, waiting for him to speak.

"I have your things in storage," he said timidly.

"What things?" I croaked.

"Mr. Lewis asked me to place all the boxes in storage for you to collect before he left," the doorman clarified, but I was still confused.

"I don't understand." I shook my head.

The doorman's eyes widened, realizing I was clueless. "Mr. Lewis moved out today—he terminated the lease at the end of last month when he finally got that big promotion—you didn't know?" He spoke softly, afraid to upset me further.

I let out a huge sigh and slumped into the nearest bench as I felt my legs tremble beneath me.

Things had been bad between us. I knew that.

I didn't have the energy to fight with him. I had been waiting for him to tell me it was over because I was too chicken shit to do it myself. I didn't think he would leave me homeless without notice, however.

And the promotion…I chuckled manically under my

breath.

Of course.

I had been so wrapped up in worrying over how to break up with him that I had never thought to ask myself why on earth he continued staying with me. We weren't having sex. With how much both of us were working, we barely saw each other. He was getting absolutely nothing out of the relationship, except a leg up at the firm.

"Are you alright, miss?" The doorman approached me cautiously.

My mind was spinning.

I had nowhere to go.

I took a deep breath.

I needed to take things one step at a time, or I was going to have a panic attack…I could feel bile rising in my throat, and I needed to calm down—to disassociate myself from what was happening.

"Do you have a dolly to help me get the boxes to my car?" I asked quietly, keeping my eyes trained on my sneakers, unable to face the doorman and his pity. I needed to take things one step at a time and focus on the tasks right in front of me.

"I'll help you—pull into the loading zone," he instructed me.

Begrudgingly, and careful to keep my balance, I got up from the bench and walked back out the doors to my car in the parking garage to pull it around the front of the building.

The doorman was kind enough to bring all the boxes to me and help me load everything.

I was surprised at the lack of belongings. I'd never been much for materialism or sentimental keepsakes, but Adam, it seemed, owned everything we had shared. I was left with two suitcases of clothes and shoes, a few small boxes of books, and another couple with toiletries and miscellaneous bits from my nightstand and around the house.

My entire life fit into my car.

I felt humiliated.

I felt defeated.

I felt so small.

With little awareness of my surroundings, I just started driving. Running through everything that had happened, everything that I needed to do to find a way out of the mess I had created, and everything that had been taken from me.

I lost time as I drove.

As consciousness returned to me, I found that I was pulling into the long driveway to Willowbrooke. It was almost midnight, and I had no recollection of how I'd gotten back to where it all started.

Not wanting anyone to see me, I turned my headlights off as I approached the roundabout in front of the house and parked the car on the very edge of the driveway, hoping that in the dark, nobody would notice it overnight. It was so late, but I could still see lights on in the house.

I was debating if it would be a better idea to sleep in

my car or try to locate a motel I could afford nearby for the night, when I was startled by the passenger door opening.

Leo West slid into the passenger seat, casting the car back into darkness as the door closed behind him, extinguishing the dash light.

We sat in silence for ages.

The only sounds were our breathing, and my occasional sniffling. I couldn't even look at Leo; I just stared at the steering wheel in a daze, wondering if I was imagining him next to me. And if he was really there, why wasn't he giving me a piece of his mind for going into the solarium against his order and then having the audacity to return, when he had been quite clear about me leaving the premises?

Leo's coat rustled as he nervously adjusted his long legs in my compact car. I heard him sigh before he spoke, his voice soft, "I'm sorry."

I froze, eyes still trained on the steering wheel.

"I was completely out of line," he continued quietly but sincerely. "I was wrong to raise my voice with you. I couldn't—I wasn't in my right mind…" he trailed off.

I remained silent.

I hadn't been expecting an apology.

I had been expecting he would demand one from me.

"I should have listened to you, instead of flying off the handle. I regretted everything the moment you were out of sight—you left so quickly, I—I'm so sorry. I'm sorry I made you cry." The words seemed to physically pain him, not because he didn't want to say them, but because they were true. He was remorseful.

"I'm not proud of myself—of my reaction. I deeply regret how I handled the situation—how awful I must have made you feel. I should have given you the benefit of the doubt. I hope you can forgive me." He sighed, as if asking for my forgiveness was too much for him to hope for.

Still stunned at the turn of events, and reeling from all that had happened, not just at Willowbrooke, I found it easy to offer my forgiveness. "I'm sorry too." I winced as my voice cracked. "Margot told me why you keep it closed—why you can't bear to be in there." I hoped I wouldn't get her in trouble.

Leo nodded solemnly.

"I let curiosity get the best of me. I should have just shut the door and told you what happened when you got back instead of investigating."

"Wait—the door—it really was open?" Leo sounded confused.

I chanced a glance over to him in the dark; only the dim light of the crescent moon illuminated the outline of his features. "Yes, and the curtains too. Someone opened all of them. I was trying to close them when you found me."

Leo's jaw clenched. "I keep the solarium locked."

"Did you think I went snooping around your room looking for a key?" I half laughed, but stopped when I realized that was exactly what he'd thought. "I didn't even know the door was locked because I haven't gone near it—or your bedroom—in the last two months, at your explicit request. I would *never* do that to you."

"I know that," Leo sighed. "I just saw red—my behavior was inexcusable—"

"I forgive you." I reached out, gently resting my palm on Leo's arm, but retracted it almost immediately when his eyes met mine in question.

A tense silence enveloped us again. But hope began to bloom in my chest. All was not lost.

Leo was the one to break the quiet for a second time. "I tried calling after I calmed down, but it went straight to voicemail. I was worried about you. What made you come back?" he asked timidly, perhaps feeling he didn't have the right to pose such a question.

A fresh wave of tears crashed over me as the impact of the evening sunk deeper into my bones. I didn't even know why I was crying. I should have been relieved that things were over with Adam and that I hadn't even had to lift a finger to make it happen.

Without another word, Leo reached across the console and took my hand in his to comfort me. His skin was warm and soft, a comforting blanket on the coldest night. Something seemed to shift between us, and my stomach fluttered hopefully.

Leo had been open with me, and now it was my turn to be vulnerable, despite my humiliation and foolishness.

When I felt capable of speaking, I exhaled, then said, "The short story is that I was moved out of my apartment and have nowhere to go."

Leo's warm hand gently squeezed mine in support. "And the long story?" he dared.

I sighed, swallowing back more tears, trying to regain some sort of composure. "The long story—the long story is that my boyfriend—or I guess now ex-boyfriend—things haven't been good between us for a while. I've been wanting to break things off, but I could never find the right words, or the right time…not that there's ever a right time." I rolled my eyes at my continued excuses.

"Why did things sour?" Leo's thumb gently began to stroke the tender skin of my hand.

"Mina says he's all talk, but no action." I smiled sardonically in the dark at her astute observation. "We met at my parents' firm. He was very charming, and things happened really fast in the beginning. But lately…" I sighed.

"He's the kind of guy who can turn things around on you. He's very flirtatious, and if I said anything he'd call me jealous and insecure. Then he'd apologize later and say he wanted to fix things. I wanted to believe him." I ran my hands over my face. "But I'm an idiot."

"No you're not. It sounds like he's been gaslighting you for a while. That's a difficult cycle to break," Leo argued, pulling both my hands back into his, silently encouraging me to continue.

I gave a humorless laugh. "Hindsight, Leo," I chided.

"I knew things were bad. He wasn't thrilled when I left the firm. The doorman said he gave notice after he got a promotion at work. Now I'm wondering if he was only with me to get ahead in his career. I've been walking on eggshells for months, but by the time I started working here, we barely spoke anymore—we were less than roommates.

"He was always out late with people at work and had constant plans on the weekends. I was never invited. But it was better when he was gone anyway." I felt the truth spilling from me. I'd been holding in so much, even from Mina.

"Why didn't you leave?" Leo asked quietly.

"I don't know. I wanted to. I tried a few times, but he'd twist what I was saying and offer to work on things—to make things better," I answered honestly. "I wasn't strong enough to be firm, and I was…scared."

I leaned back into my seat, careful not to sever the physical connection with Leo. His warmth was the only thing tethering me to reality.

"That's—a lot," he managed, shifting in his seat so his shoulder touched mine across the console. "I'm so sorry."

"I had nowhere else to go. Mina is out of the country for the next two weeks and doesn't have room at her place anyway. My parents haven't spoken to me since I left the firm in September. Sloan—my sister," I clarified, "she has room and would let me stay for a day or two, but would immediately rat me out to my parents, and I can't take them saying 'I told you so'—I might actually murder them if I heard them say it one more time."

"And I don't know if I even still have a job." I grimaced, addressing the elephant in the room.

"Of course you do," Leo said without hesitation. "If you're still willing to put up with me, that is. I promise to never raise my voice with you again. Ever."

"Thank you." I sniffled, feeling a huge sense of relief at the confirmation. I might have been homeless, but at least I wasn't completely destitute.

"And don't be ridiculous—you'll stay here, with me," Leo said, as if it was the most obvious thing in the world, despite it being an invitation I never imagined I'd receive.

"Leo—I couldn't impose on you like that," I argued. "It's going to take me forever to find a local rental I can afford—"

"Penny," Leo stopped me.

I looked up at him.

"I should have been more clear. I'd like for you to stay here for the duration of the project."

My lips parted involuntarily.

"I don't know why I didn't think of it sooner." He gave a wry smile. "You'd be doing me a favor, after all—less of a commute means I'll have more of your time at my disposal."

His reasoning was paper-thin. But I knew better than to argue.

I had no other options. He was throwing me a much needed lifeline.

I could still look for something nearby on the off chance I found a place in my price range…which I knew damn well was going to be impossible.

"And besides," he continued, "it'll be nice to have some company."

With that, he released my hand from his. I immediately felt the loss of his warmth and comfort.

"Pop the trunk," he instructed as he got out of the car.

Without thinking, I obeyed, and watched silently as he grabbed two boxes and carried them toward the house. I hadn't even agreed to his offer, but he had made the choice for me.

I followed quickly behind, dragging my suitcase across the gravel.

CHAPTER 5

SUFFOCATING

Leo and I decided what we referred to as the "pink room" upstairs would be the best place for me, at least for a little while. We were planning on playing a bit of musical chairs with the furniture when the flooring restoration started, and the pink room was the last on the plan. Until then, I'd have the whole floor to myself, which felt right from a privacy perspective for both Leo and me.

The first night, Leo lugged all of my boxes into the dining room so I'd have easy access to pull out anything I needed urgently, but the rest would be out of the way enough not to bother either of us, or the construction workers. Laughing at my slow pace up the stairs, Leo wrestled my large suitcase away from me, and took it the rest of the way up.

I crashed so hard in that pink frilly canopy bed the first night. Physically exhausted from driving for hours on end and mentally exhausted from the roller coaster of a day I'd had, I was dead to the world within moments of my head hitting the pillow.

The initial couple days were a mix of awkwardness and odd familiarity as we shared the space twenty-four seven. After all, I had worked there for two months; I knew all the nooks and crannies pretty well by then, but I had rarely been at the house after dark. And in the evenings, the house took on a whole new sinister demeanor—one that I tried very hard to ignore.

At night, shadows stretched longer, the smallest noises echoed louder, and my imagination was intent on playing tricks on me around every corner. I couldn't get the conversation I'd had with Margot out of my mind, knowing that in the last few decades alone, more than a couple people had passed in and around the property.

I thought back to my first impression of Willowbrooke, the day of my interview. I had told Mina I thought the place looked haunted, and I'd meant it. And now I was witnessing firsthand how the space ebbed and flowed between day and night—how it moved around its inhabitants, perhaps waiting for another soul to add to its collection…

Each morning I would wake up to the same fresh cup of coffee waiting on the counter and Leo across from me, ready to hear what we had in store for the day. The counter at that point was a makeshift coffee bar I had cobbled together on a side table I'd brought into the living room from upstairs.

The ritual that had developed between Leo and I from the beginning of the project had long been the highlight of my day, and I'd spent most of my morning commute scripting what I would review with Leo and looking forward to the bitter steaming dark liquid I knew would be ready for me upon my arrival.

While our morning procedure largely stayed the same, without my long commute, we could start work over an hour earlier, which now included us taking our coffee to the living room and watching the tail end of the sunrise over the oceanside cliffs beyond the back lawn. Although Leo had always opened the curtains before my arrival, I began to take on the task myself, while he tended to the coffee machine.

"Val gets the coffee from a local place; they get fair-trade beans directly and grind the beans in-store," Leo told me one morning a couple weeks into the project, after I had asked about the unlabeled black bag of coffee grounds. Every now and then I'd get glimpses of the Leo that hid behind his self-built walls, keeping everyone and every emotion out, but also keeping himself locked away inside. I'd made a note that day that coffee was something that was important to Leo.

Whether it was the liquid itself, the caffeine boost, or simply the morning ritual of it all, our first sips together every morning were a quiet moment of zen that I never took for granted. The brief spark of sheer joy on Leo's face when he saw the coffee station I'd put together was well worth the effort. It was a lesson that paying very close attention and becoming attuned to his almost imperceptible shifts in mood or emotion would pay off eventually.

Having dealt with Adam's mercurial mood swings for a long time, I was used to ferreting out the smallest indications of how a person might react, or how their perception of an interaction would play out. Leo's reactions, or lack thereof, were much more diminutive, but I was slowly learning his quirks. Try as he might, he couldn't keep me out forever. I was determined to build a friendship between us, yet whether he wanted to count me as a friend or not was up to him.

I tried to ignore the small voice inside that suggested he could become something more than a friend. Those thoughts were the hardest to evade. The hope that came with them was even worse.

It only took a matter of days, staying at the house full-time, for Leo's walls to very slowly start crumbling. So gradual was the progress, that I doubted he was even aware of it happening.

"C'mon, use your muscles, Pen," Leo chided as I struggled to help him move a heavy chest of drawers from one room to the other as we prepared for the flooring work to begin. He had been teasing me more lately and had taken to calling me by a nickname when it suited him. I didn't mind. Mina was the only one who usually called me "Pen" for short.

My family wouldn't dare use the moniker. It had, after all, taken them years as a teenager to convince them that I preferred to be called Penny instead of my full name: Penelope. It was an old family name which my parents had fallen in love with, never considering their daughter would have to live with the name for the rest of her life, whether she liked it or not.

I hated being called Penelope, but Penny...I felt like a Penny, and when Mina, or now Leo, used the shorthand version, it made me feel warm and fuzzy inside. The implied familiarity from Leo made me nervous...but the good kind of nervous. It was a secret code being shared amongst allies. I didn't think either of them knew how endearing it felt to me. Maybe I didn't have to tell them—they could probably see it on my face.

Late afternoon the second day after I moved in, I caught Leo mindlessly scrolling through the stock artwork on the new frame TV, which could mimic the look of artwork when the TV wasn't in use.

When Leo asked my preferences, it sparked a great debate that culminated in an empty wine bottle split between the two of us, and a disagreement over modern and abstract art versus more traditional styles. I wasn't a fan of the former, but he disagreed. I suspected Leo didn't like modern art either, but it seemed he enjoyed playing devil's advocate and pushing my buttons.

But after the debate, I found that most days Leo chose

artwork that was well within my personal preferences, typically classical subjects in a baroque or rococo style. He liked to try a new piece every day.

If I didn't know any better, I'd think I was growing on him.

Evenings at the house were a little bit awkward. Leo was still cranky since the kitchen wasn't accessible, so once we'd eaten our second meal of the day, which Leo would order in, I'd make a quick retreat to the pink room, not wanting to disrupt whatever normal nighttime routine Leo had. As far as I was concerned, I wanted him to forget I existed outside normal working hours, so he didn't feel as though his space was being invaded.

Regardless of my tactics, we would occasionally have fleeting run-ins, but I avoided him as much as possible. Still, I had to admit to myself that it was nice to see a different side to Leo. After hours, he was a bit more relaxed, but also a bit more morose. Most nights, he'd post up in the living room with a glass of wine and read.

Although I had argued it would be better to wait to order the new sofa with all the construction in the house, he couldn't stand the floral monstrosity any longer and practically begged me to order it early. It was nice to see he was putting it to good use. The deep cognac leather sectional fit well in the space, and I was excited for how the whole room would look when everything was put together.

Seeing him out of work-mode was both comforting, but

also disquieting. I could feel myself being pulled to him. I had to remind myself with increasing frequency that it was simply a line I could not cross. But the more Leo came out of his shell around me, the more I found myself thinking of him and what it would be like to be with someone like him…or just him.

I was playing a dangerous game.

William stopped by mid-week to share a glass of wine with Leo in the library. The two of them were awfully secretive, which had me wondering if they were conspiring against me. But contrary to my conspiracy theories, William pulled me aside to apologize for not stepping in the day Leo had found me in the solarium.

"What could you have done?" I shook my head, waving off his apology.

"I could have said something—I should have." He frowned. "It weighed heavily on me after you left, and once the shock had subsided, I gave Leo a piece of my mind about how he had handled the situation."

So that's why Leo had displayed such a quick turnaround.

It didn't make his apology any less genuine, but it did explain why he'd felt so tortured about how I'd left the house that day.

"I appreciate what you did," I thanked him.

"I'm glad you've decided to stay." William's admission surprised me.

"Oh?" I managed in response.

"Leo's been alone too long—I think it'll be good for him to have you around." William smiled gently. "He's different with you."

"Hopefully in a good way." I laughed awkwardly.

William joined me. "Yes, in a good way." He chuckled. "Take care of him." His tone was still jovial, but the message was sobering.

"I will," I promised, giving him a small wave as he took his leave.

Margot joined us for lunch on Thursday. I'm not sure what I thought her reaction to the new living arrangement would be, but she appeared delighted at the idea.

"You're always so generous and thoughtful, Leo," she gushed over her salad. "I raised you well."

As I had come to expect with Margot, she got a little too deep a little too quickly, when she asked if I had any family to stay with.

Leo looked up at me across the table, silently giving me permission to circumvent the truth if it was uncomfortable. But I feared Margot would sniff out any lies or half-truths, so I was honest.

I explained my recent estrangement with my family after leaving the firm, and how my sister and I had never really been close because our parents had pitted us against each other…a silly gambit because everyone had known Sloan would win, whatever the contest was.

"I know it's hard, honey, but don't close that door if you can manage. Look at what happened with Leo and George." Margot took a sip of her sparkling water.

Leo held his breath, waiting to see how much Margot would divulge. After I'd confessed to knowing why the solarium was kept closed because Margot had spilled the beans, he had to know that wasn't the only thing we'd spoken about. But I wasn't about to give Leo a full debrief of our lunch conversation.

"Thank goodness my prodding worked on both of them—if they hadn't reconciled…" She reached across the table and took Leo's hand in hers. "You would have regretted it for the rest of your life."

Leo looked a mix of a broken little boy, unsure if the acceptance he was hearing was true, and the grown man who was broken in a different way, still grieving the loss of the father he barely knew, and now, never would.

Her gaze held his for a long moment. I thought she might have forgotten I was in the room, but then she retracted her hand from Leo's as she cleared her throat.

"You might consider talking to your sister as well. Maybe as adults you can find common ground. George and I had a difficult relationship growing up—it's not easy feeling inferior your whole life. But I'm glad we worked through our childhood to see that our differences were an artifact of the way we were brought up, not because he and I didn't get along," Margot commented.

I couldn't even remember the last time I had talked to Sloan—more than just passing words anyway. The apple of my parents' eye, she had gone to school to be a structural engineer and was being groomed to take over the firm when my parents were ready to retire in the next ten or so years.

Sloan was the opposite of me in so many ways. Where I was short, freckled, amber-haired, and tomboyish, she was tall, willowy, feminine, with curves in all the right places, and long naturally blonde hair. The only feature we shared was our blue eyes, and if we hadn't had that in common, I would truly have looked the part of the red-headed step child. I was treated like one, so our identical gaze didn't seem to matter much.

Where I had failed and struggled in school, she had excelled and was top of whatever class she was in. My parents constantly sang her praises, and more than once, I'd heard them begrudgingly lament why I couldn't be more like her. They had no idea how devastating that treatment had been for me at such a formative age. I didn't think I could ever get past it—no amount of therapy in the world could squash those kinds of issues.

It wasn't even until meeting Mina in college that I'd realized how abnormal my treatment had been, and I had slowly started trying to wake from the haze I had been drifting through my entire adolescence.

Sloan and I had never been close. She was always so quiet, obedient, and bookish. We had nothing in common. If I called her that exact moment, I wouldn't have even known what to talk to her about.

But Margot wasn't wrong.

I'd grown up with Sloan, but I didn't know a single thing about her as an adult, other than her profession and place of work. Granted, she hadn't tried to connect with me either, but maybe she'd gone through a similarly traumatizing experience growing up, which had kept her so compliant. I resolved to reach out and give her the benefit of the doubt. The worst-case scenario was that things stayed as icy as they currently were, and I was fine with that arrangement as well.

Had Leo seen a fellow tortured soul in me the day of the interview? Had he asked me to take the project sight unseen because he'd seen himself in me? Both our parents had pushed us away and shaped us into perfect little humans filled with self-hatred and crippling doubt.

Could we overcome our fate?

Or were we doomed to succumb to self-fulfilling prophecies?

I had been staying at Willowbrooke for just under a week when more odd occurrences began to happen.

At first it was just little things, like my door being left open when I was sure that I had closed it, or the curtains being drawn when I knew for certain I had pulled them open that morning. But then it escalated when I continued to be awakened in the middle of the night by a singular thump, at exactly 2:13 a.m., coming from the crawl space above the pink room.

I was hesitant to mention any of it to Leo because he had been somewhat dismissive of my earlier claims of a potential haunting. Even I had to admit to myself that I sounded a bit neurotic about the whole ordeal, but part of me wished he had given my concerns more validation.

While I didn't *not* believe in the supernatural, I was definitely skeptical in most circumstances. But in this case, where I was the one experiencing numerous things and was starting to feel a bit unraveled, it was easier to consider a paranormal source, when the alternative was me losing my mind.

It was the fourth night in a row that I had been awoken by the thump, at the exact same time as the previous three nights, that I sat up in bed, fearful and unable to get back to sleep. I could feel anxiety rising in me; my stomach was in knots.

Seeing a sliver of moonlight streaming through a crack in the curtains, I drowsily made my way over to the window to peek outside at the lawn below. The sight that met me sent me stumbling backward, tripping into the bed.

Walking across the lawn was a woman in a white nightgown, long dark hair flowing down her back. Her feet were bare. She had to have been freezing, as the temperature was well into the 30s at that time of night—or rather, early morning.

The woman's steps were slow and methodical as she crossed diagonally through the lawn toward the cliff. And when I thought of the cliff, it dawned on me that although I couldn't see her face, she looked familiar.

Shortly after arriving back at Willowbrooke, Margot had stolen me one afternoon to show me a family album in the library. We had spent over an hour together as she'd prattled on over adorable baby photos of Leo with his parents. The woman below reminded me of someone I had seen in those faded photographs taken decades ago. She had an identical figure and hair to Leo's mother, Christine.

I went back over to the window, and the figure was gone. But she'd already been so close to the cliff when I'd seen her. She could have jumped. If I really was seeing a specter repeat her last moments, or if it was a real person, maybe a neighbor sleepwalking, she could have found cover in the tree line, which offered little visibility past the first stand of willow trees, even in the late fall, with their lack of leaves— the branches were too thick and too many, with the trees clustered so close together.

I was debating on what to do, feeling my heart pounding in my chest, when a clatter from downstairs sent me absolutely over the edge. Had the woman made it inside the house? I had no idea how heavy or light of a sleeper Leo was; would he have heard the noise? He'd never mentioned the thumps, but they were coming from two floors above him, so even if he was a light sleeper, the chances of him hearing them were slim.

The uncomfortable feeling in the pit of my stomach had spread to every part of me, making my fingers and toes feel numb, save for the thrumming of my rapid heartbeat.

Something was very wrong—I was scared. But I felt a sudden and overwhelming need to find Leo. I couldn't stand to be alone in the dark any longer.

So, very slowly and as quietly as I could muster, I made my way down the main staircase to the ground floor, hoping that whatever, or whoever, had made the noise was already gone, or wouldn't hear me approach.

I realized halfway down the stairs, when I saw a dim light from the kitchen, that I hadn't thought through a plan at all. Was I going to confront the intruder or try to sneak past to find Leo in his room?

After another few steps, I froze when I saw a figure illuminated by the kitchen light, behind the translucent plastic sheeting that Danny had put up to make sure dust and dirt particles from the construction wouldn't contaminate the rest of the house. Again, I could hear my heart pounding in my ears, so loudly that I wondered if the intruder could hear it as well.

Another clatter caused me to stumble backwards on the stairs, shocked by the noise. Followed by the figure cursing at the noise he had caused. And upon hearing the voice behind the plastic curtain, I realized it wasn't an intruder; it was Leo.

I took a deep breath, trying to calm whatever was left of my nerves, and made my way over to the sheeting, pulling it back to approach Leo. The crinkling of the plastic must have shocked him because he dropped his bowl again, scattering pretzels across the newly installed tile flooring.

Leo spun around, a gasp hanging from his lips and his hand over his heart. "Jesus, Pen, you scared the shit out of me." He gulped.

I paused, taking Leo in for a brief moment. He was wearing charcoal gray sweatpants, a white crew neck shirt, and slippers. I realized I'd never seen him out of his regular uniform of well-tailored slacks and crisp button-up shirts, always complete with a pair of shiny lace-up shoes. He was handsome and put together no matter what he wore, it would seem.

"Well, you scared me first," I accused him. "What are you doing up in the middle of the night?" I realized I had no right asking him what he did in his own house, but the sentiment arrived too late for me to retract the question.

"I—" He paused, weighing if he should tell me the truth or only part of it. "I have insomnia," he admitted.

"Oh." I winced. "I'm sorry." I wasn't sure if that was the right thing to say, but it felt right in the moment.

Leo waved a hand to dismiss the thought, telling me not to worry about him without saying it aloud. "I'm sorry about the noise—a bowl fell out of the cabinet, and then I slipped on the tile—and then you—scared the shit out of me." He sighed as he began to pick up the broken pretzel fragments from the ground, placing them back into the bowl.

"I was awake before I heard you…" I admitted.

Leo looked up from where he was crouched in the middle of the kitchen. "Are you alright?" He seemed to sense that something was amiss.

"I saw someone outside—a woman, walking across the lawn…to the cliff." I had debated whether I should say the last bit, but if I had seen a real person, they might be injured or in danger.

Leaving half the pretzels on the ground, Leo set the bowl on the counter and said, "Show me," as he motioned for me to lead the way.

I crossed the living room and pulled back the drawn curtain covering the glass door that led to the back patio and lawn. There was no one within sight. "I swear I didn't imagine it."

Leo didn't reply, but gently nudged past me to unlock and open the door, letting in a gust of freezing air in the process.

Instinctively, my arms wrapped around my chest to brace myself from the cold. I stayed inside, but watched Leo tread across the stone patio to the edge of the grass, where he abruptly stopped.

"Come back inside; it's too cold out," I called to him in

a half whisper.

"C'mere." He beckoned me outside.

I grimaced as I stepped over the threshold; my socks immediately felt soggy as I crossed the damp patio toward Leo. When I made it next to him, he pointed a few yards away, where I could see marks in the dewy grass.

"What is that?" I squinted in the barely-there moonlight.

"Footsteps," Leo said.

I blanched.

I knew I had seen the woman from my bedroom window, but I think there was a part of me that assumed I had been seeing things.

"Go get your coat and some shoes," Leo instructed.

Making haste, I did as I was told and met Leo back downstairs, where he had also swapped his slippers for a pair of worn sneakers and a large black wool peacoat. He handed me a heavy-duty flashlight, matching the one he held in his own hands. The cold metal of the flashlight bit into my fingers.

Following alongside the set of footprints, we slowly made our way across the lawn. The depressions in the grass ended right at the cliffside, which perturbed both of us.

"Stay here," Leo said before walking right up to the edge, gently crouching down, and lying flat on his stomach in the dirt to peek over the edge of the cliff. Surely his light wouldn't penetrate all the way down to the coast, but there might have been just enough moonlight to see if there was someone at the bottom.

Leo shook his head before delicately extricating himself from the ground, brushing off the dirt from his coat. "Nothing," he said.

Placing a gentle hand on the small of my back, Leo escorted me into the house, where he took one last wary glance across the lawn before locking the door and drawing the curtains closed once more.

"I told you Willowbrooke is haunted," I stated half-joking, half-serious.

"Don't be ridiculous." Leo shook his head.

"Then what do you think it was?" I asked, mildly upset that he still didn't believe me. Either way, there was evidence that something was going on, supernatural or not.

"Maybe it was from Carl..." Leo speculated, needing a logical explanation. "He was here today. Maybe the grass where he walked made the dew appear differently..." We both knew he was grasping at straws.

I wanted to say, "But why did the footprints go to the edge and disappear?" or "What about the woman?" Instead, I quietly muttered, "Maybe..." to appease him. Joking about the house being haunted was one thing, but the reality of it felt too distressing to dwell on.

An uncomfortable silence fell between us.

Leo broke first. "The woman you saw..." he said quietly, "what did she look like?"

"She was barefoot, wearing a sleeveless white nightgown

that went to her ankles. She was short—not much taller than me, slight frame, with long dark hair—the moonlight reflected off her, and her hair moved in the wind…" I remembered as I spoke, tugging at my mind for other small details, but none materialized. "I swear she was real."

Leo pursed his lips, maybe he had been hoping I'd be more descriptive, or that hearing what I'd seen would make him suddenly realize what was actually going on.

"And…she looked like your mom." I heard my small voice escape me, before I realized the impact of what I'd said.

Leo's jaw clenched at the mention of his mother. He remained silent.

I felt dread building in the pit of my stomach. I'd overstepped. I felt awful.

"I'm sorry," I breathed. But it was too late.

"Go back to bed, Penny," Leo commanded flatly.

"Leo…" I reached out to him, but he flinched away from my touch.

Swallowing the lump in my throat, I relented, leaving him brooding in the dark living room, not daring to look back as I made my way upstairs to my room.

I didn't sleep.

I knew things would be tepid between Leo and I the next day.

What I didn't anticipate was that he would avoid me

entirely. How was I supposed to clear the air if he couldn't even stand to be in the same house with me, let alone the same room?

For the first time since starting the project, I wasn't greeted with Leo and a fresh cup of coffee upon waking. Instead I ran into Danny and his crew, who were starting early, as the kitchen was almost complete—only missing some finishing, but critical touches.

"Where's…Leo?" I asked, confused.

"Went into town—said to tell you he'll be gone most of the day," Danny grumbled, annoyed to be playing messenger. "Lover's spat?" He waggled his eyebrows, teasing.

I rolled my eyes in response. "Hardly." I scowled, making my way over to the coffee station, where there was exactly enough for one cup left warming in the glass carafe…he hadn't forgotten me after all. I felt my cheeks redden at the thought, and then my blush deepened, embarrassed that it pleased me so much.

Does Leo think of me as much as I think of him?

"Are you still on track to finish tomorrow?" I asked Danny, while pouring the steaming coffee into my usual mug.

"As long as you don't have any more last-minute changes," he growled.

"It was *one* thing—it's not my fault they delivered the wrong tone of hardware." I shook my head, knowing that Danny was joking, but also knowing that he'd never let me live down the mistake, as if I had packed the wrong parts in the box myself.

"Someone got crumbs all over the floor. You know anything about that?" Danny glared at me.

I threw my hands up defensively. "It wasn't me," I said honestly, leaving out the part where I had seen Leo commit the offense the night before. "I'll be upstairs moving furniture if you need me."

"I'll send a couple guys up in a bit to help you—just need them for a little longer," Danny offered.

"Thank you." I smiled, and carefully made my way up the back stairs.

The flooring guys were finally available to start refinishing the hardwoods, after they had rescheduled multiple times due to other jobs running longer, which didn't bode well for my project timeline. Danny insisted that they ran late because they did quality work and wouldn't leave a job until it was perfect.

Danny's endorsement was enough for me to swallow my pride and growing anxiety over the timeline extending well past the holidays. Leo seemed ambivalent about the delay, and frankly, about the holidays in general.

Just before lunch, one of the workmen who had been helping me came back upstairs from a quick break and told me Margot was downstairs with a woman he didn't recognize.

Confused by Margot's unexpected appearance with a guest, I trotted down the steps, hoping I wouldn't be judged too harshly in my workout leggings, an old paint-splattered shirt, grubby sneakers, and a sweaty disposition from moving all the furniture on the second floor into the round master above the solarium.

"Hi Margot," I greeted Leo's aunt. "We weren't expecting you today; Leo's out running errands," I told her, not sure that he was actually doing so.

Margot's laugh tinkled as she said, "I didn't know I needed an appointment to come and go from my own home."

"I'm sorry," I apologized instinctively. "It's just a messy day, is all."

"Don't worry, dear, we'll only be a moment," Margot said. "This is Miss Hawthorne." She stepped to her right, allowing me to see the beautiful young woman that had been standing behind her.

The woman couldn't have been any older than me, perhaps in her late twenties. Her flawless pale skin was juxtaposed by her dark hair, pulled back into a sleek bun at the crown of her head.

I didn't have to see the labels on her clothes, purse, or shoes to know they were designer. If I didn't know Margot was childless, I would have mistaken the woman for her daughter, for her taste in apparel alone.

"Nice to meet you." She smiled sweetly, and extended her hand to shake mine. I would have found it odd that she didn't share her first name, but occasionally Margot was overly formal, so I disregarded the thought. And honestly, there was much I didn't know about people at Margot's level of affluence; maybe this was common?

"Oh." I looked down at her hand, then at mine. "I would—I don't want to get you dirty." I could feel my face heating. I would have worn my usual jeans-shirt-blazer combo if I'd known we'd have company.

"It's alright." She beamed, her politeness disarming me.

"Did you need something in particular, Margot?" I asked, trying to be helpful.

"Actually, Miss Hawthorne just moved back to the area," Margot began.

"I grew up here," the young woman clarified.

I nodded tentatively.

"We've been busy planning a charity gala in George's honor, and she mentioned she was looking to decorate her new home. Naturally, I told her how well Leo's renovations were coming along while we were at brunch this morning, and since she didn't have any afternoon plans, I thought we'd stop by so she could see for herself."

"Oh," I felt even more embarrassed. "Well, did you have any questions about the project? We still have quite a ways to go," I admitted.

"I can see that—but the kitchen…what an improvement." Miss Hawthorne marveled at the open kitchen behind her. "I'm impressed."

"We've got a great contractor." I smiled at Danny, who was busy concentrating on fixing grout lines to his level of perfection.

"Do you have a business card?" Miss Hawthorne asked genuinely.

"I don't." My face fell. "But I'll still be working on this project for a while. I'm sure Leo wouldn't mind if you stopped by—if you have any questions."

"I'm sure he wouldn't," Margot agreed, smiling at Miss Hawthorne.

"I'm opening up a gallery in town in the new year," Miss Hawthorne told me. "You'll have to come visit some time."

"Of course," I agreed without thinking.

"We'll let ourselves out," Margot informed me, which was her nice way of telling me to get lost.

"I'll be in touch." Miss Hawthorne gave me a small wave, her jewelry sparkling in the sunlight.

"Have a nice day, ladies." I gave one last curt smile before heading back upstairs, feeling awkward about the entire exchange. I thought Leo might have minded his aunt bringing over a stranger—but then again, she'd mentioned the kitchen being an improvement, so maybe she'd been there before. If she'd grown up in the area, perhaps she knew Leo.

Carefully stepping over the giant pile of linens we planned to donate or discard, I made myself busy helping the workmen move the rest of the furniture. The only things that remained were the bedframe and nightstand in the pink room. I had planned on sleeping on the couch for a few days while they worked upstairs, but since learning that Leo would likely be up most nights, due to his insomnia, I'd have to work out a different plan with him, whenever he deigned to return.

Leo didn't get back until almost six that evening, bringing a bag of takeout food with him. "I just got your usual," he said quietly, before making a beeline for the library with his dinner.

He remembered my order…

The first waft of my favorite ramen order hit me like a ton of bricks. I hadn't realized how hungry I'd been because I was worried about where Leo had been all day and anxious that he was mad at me for bringing up his mom when he'd never said much to me about her before.

Everything I knew about Christine was from Margot, and I wasn't sure I was even supposed to know as much as I did. If I hadn't been so tired and so frightened the night before, maybe I would have had more sense than to suggest that her freaking ghost was haunting the backyard. "Idiot…" I mumbled to myself.

After enjoying every last bit of my dinner, I waited around the kitchen for a while, hoping that maybe Leo would come back out to throw away his food container; he'd never leave it in the library. But when he still hadn't returned after an hour or so, I sighed, knowing that I'd have to risk angering him further by finding him first.

Slowly, quietly, I made my way to the library.

The door was open just a crack, enough for me to hear the tail end of a conversation Leo was having. I couldn't hear what he was saying, and frankly, I didn't want to because I had come to make sure we were okay, not violate his privacy further. But it was clear whatever he was talking about, he was upset.

When I was sure the call had ended, I rapped lightly on the door, pushing it open just enough to peek around it. "Leo?" I asked quietly.

Leo was sitting at the desk at the far end of the library, his shoulders hunched over. Whatever the call had been about… Leo seemed distraught.

He looked up, his eyes pained when they met mine. "It's okay. You can come in," he said.

"Are you alright?" I wasn't sure what was going on, but I knew he wasn't okay.

"What did you need, Penny?" He ignored my question.

"I came to apologize about last night." I approached the desk cautiously, unsure of what kind of response I would receive.

Leo's brow furrowed. "Apologize?"

"What I said about…" I didn't want to say it out loud, but Leo didn't seem to understand. "…about your mom…" I said the last words so quietly I barely heard myself, but Leo definitely heard me.

He sighed. "Have you thought I was upset with you all day?" Leo somehow saw right through me.

I was frozen. "You—missed coffee," I stuttered.

"I left you a cup," he said defensively. "I'm not mad at you. I had an early meeting—I should have said something yesterday, but I forgot."

"Okay," I replied, unsure of what else to say.

Leo raked his hand through his hair as he stood. He turned away from me to look out the window toward the cliffside. It was a cloudy night, so not much could be seen beyond the illumination of the outdoor house lights.

"Maybe you were right about this place being haunted," Leo murmured. "But if there's anyone haunting this house, it's surely my father."

Surprised by his admission, I could only ask, "Why?" as I approached him at the window.

"Restoring the house wasn't my father's only request on his deathbed, you know." Leo fiddled with a tassel on the curtains. "He also asked that a private autopsy be conducted after his death."

I stayed silent, knowing that it would be inappropriate for me to interrupt Leo's confession. He was rarely this vulnerable with me, but I would be there for him, whatever he was about to confide in me.

"It turns out, it wasn't the cancer that got him in the end—he was close, but not quite there yet. The forensic pathologists said there was strong evidence he was… suffocated." Leo's voice trembled as he shared his discovery.

"And they're sure?" It seemed so out of left field.

"I've gotten several opinions, and they've all come back with the same findings." He sighed. "The one I met with today said I need to stop looking for more opinions and face the truth."

"Leo…" I breathed. I didn't know what to say.

Leo turned to me then. "Penny—you're the only person in this house I can trust." His face was solemn, but resolute.

"Why me?" I said quietly.

"Because I didn't even know you at the time—whatever happened to my father, I know you weren't involved," he told me. "You also seem to be incapable of lying to me, much to your detriment."

I couldn't help but give a short, humorless chuckle at that. He was right. I was a terrible liar at the best of times, but I also wondered if he knew that even if I could lie to him, I wouldn't want to. I only ever wanted to be honest with Leo.

"I'm so sorry," I told him.

"I know."

Seeing Leo standing there so broken and alone, I did the only thing I could think to do to comfort him…I hugged him.

I was surprised when Leo returned the embrace, holding me tightly to him, as if he hadn't been hugged in ages…and perhaps he hadn't.

CHAPTER 6

LAST DAYS

After Leo's confession in the library, I was worried that the the reality check he'd received about his father's death would drag him into a deeper hole than he already seemed to be in.

But if there was one thing that could lift his spirits, it was the grand reveal of the completed and newly renovated kitchen. With the installation of the delayed, but well worth it, top of the line appliances, the space had been completely transformed.

"All new appliances, quartz countertops, brand new bespoke shaker cabinetry, vintage aged brass hardware, and antique, reclaimed tiling." I touched each piece as I spoke.

"Welcome to your new kitchen." I smiled at Leo.

"It's really something." He gazed lovingly at the details, running his fingertips across the stunning one-of-a-kind countertop that he had scavenged from a stone yard an hour away. The veining brought out the colors in the tiling, some flecks of metallic coloring called out to the hardware, and the base ivory color went perfectly with the cabinetry paint.

"You've outdone yourself for sure." Leo grinned at me. "And you too, Danny." He turned his attention to the construction foreman, who was uncharacteristically quiet. "I can't wait to see what the two of you do with the rest of the house—if the kitchen is any indication, I've got the right people for the job."

"I'll be back next week to work with the flooring guys," Danny told Leo.

"Sure you won't stay for dinner?" Leo had invited Danny to stay, as a thank you, but Danny had politely declined.

"Thank you, sir, but I've got to get home to my family." The jolly contractor gave us both a brief wave before heading out.

"You must feel relieved to have a little of your space back." I leaned over the kitchen counter, resting my chin in my palms.

"You have no idea." Leo sighed contentedly as he began to open up the cupboards, searching for things. "But it was worth the wait."

"What are you looking for—I tried to organize things for

you, but we can move them around wherever you want." I ducked around Leo, trying to help him.

"Danny may not be staying, but I'm making *you* dinner," Leo stated.

I had figured Leo would want to cook something right away, but the thought of him cooking for me made me blush, and the flutter in my stomach returned as well. "Tell me what you need."

"I'm making pasta from scratch and marinara sauce. Val already picked up fresh tomatoes and a few other things for me."

"What do you need from the pantry?" I asked.

Leo rattled off a list of items, and I went about retrieving each of them, explaining my organizational system for the kitchen as I went. He nodded along as I pointed to the different sections.

"Apron?" Leo requested, as I tried to order all the items we had pulled out on the countertop.

"On the hook, behind the storage room door," I told him. "What can I help with?" I wasn't a great cook, but I was good at following instructions.

"Actually, I've been thinking about what we talked about in the library last night." Leo tied the black apron around his waist; it looked adorable on him.

"Oh?" I was surprised to hear him bring up the subject so nonchalantly.

"Can I run some theories past you? I think a fresh

perspective on everything would be helpful." He wiped down the counter with a wet rag, then went back over a second time with paper towels to dry the space before using a measuring cup to dump some flour directly onto the new quartz.

"Of course."

"I'd like to start from the beginning—it may get a little morbid, I suppose," he warned.

I thought maybe having this conversation while he was focused on the task at hand helped him disassociate from the fact that he was talking about his father being murdered.

"Can you give me a little more background about your father?" I asked nervously.

Leo glanced up at me after cracking his last egg over the mound of flour. "I thought Aunt Margot gossiped with you about everything," he teased.

"She told me a little, but I'd like to hear your side—your experience," I clarified.

"What exactly did Margot tell you?"

"That you didn't get along with your dad growing up, and that you had a falling out after high school and spent years away, building your own consulting business without his help," I recounted. "But then, when he got sick, Margot said she convinced you to come back and reconcile with him. So you spent the last year with him—dropped everything to take care of him." I watched Leo mixing together the eggs and flour on the counter. "That was a very selfless thing to do…"

Leo's gaze met mine for a brief moment, but then returned to his task. "Did she tell you why we fell out?"

"No."

"He told me he'd changed his will to disinherit me, that he didn't think I was grateful for everything he'd done for me growing up. I didn't realize being an absent parent had taken so much from him." Leo chuckled to himself.

"At the time, I was furious. I grew up thinking that I'd at least have a head start, with college being paid for, but Margot was the one kind enough to pick up the tab. I'm still not quite sure what I did growing up to make him hate me so much." Leo kneaded the dough roughly, as if taking out his aggression from his childhood on the ball of pasta.

"Margot said it was because of your mom…" I had debated revealing more, but if Leo really was clueless as to the reason, perhaps knowing would help.

Leo stopped abruptly and looked at me, his brow knit. "What about her?"

"She said you reminded him too much of her, that he was devastated to be around you."

Leo shook his head. "Of course I understand he never recovered after losing her, but to take it out on a child, that is something I will never understand." He resumed his kneading.

"But you did reconcile with your dad…didn't you talk about why you left…get some kind of closure about any of it?" I asked.

Leo chuckled. "Sometimes I forget you never met him. My dad never looked back. We never talked about what happened. He never apologized. But I knew him well enough not to expect anything. I came home just as much for him as I did for myself. Margot was right that I'd regret it if I didn't. I didn't expect that as an adult, as someone who made something from practically nothing, without his help, that I had managed to earn a shred of respect from the old man."

"Did you get *any* closure before he passed?" I asked out of pure curiosity.

"Sure I did," Leo said wryly. "My dad was never going to change; he expected everyone around him to adapt instead. So I adapted. But once I let go of the notion that he would suddenly become this loving father figure that I had wanted growing up, I allowed myself to start a completely fresh relationship with him. It wasn't one of father and son, but one of simple mutual respect." Leo formed the dough into a round ball.

"He respected that I made it without his help and came back to take care of him. And I respected him for standing his ground and not compromising, even when he was in a very vulnerable state." Leo tucked a piece of plastic wrap around the dough ball. "We'll work on the marinara sauce while that rests, but first I need to clean up this mess." He gestured to the flour coating the counter and his apron.

"I can clean up," I offered, hopping off the barstool across the counter from Leo. "You start prepping your sauce ingredients."

"Thanks." Leo wiped his hands on his apron and started to gather everything on a clean spot on the counter next to me.

"That must have been difficult, when you were young, to process being cut out of his will, trying to land on your feet. You must have felt alone." I was selfishly using Leo's openness to try to glean more information about his past. I wanted to know him on a deeper level.

"I was young and stupid, so yeah, I was angry for a long time, but I managed to channel that anger into motivation to succeed in school and business. I wanted to prove him wrong at first, but then after a while, and a lot of therapy, I realized that it was more important to prove to myself that I could manage on my own.

"I'd been doing it my whole life anyway, but to have something tangible, like a degree from an Ivy-league and a lucrative business, that felt more real," Leo admitted. "The day I got to pay Margot back for my tuition and William back for his initial startup investment, those were good days." He smiled to himself.

"You're very resilient," I observed.

Leo gave me a small smile. "Thanks," he replied bashfully.

"So you'd been away for years—"

"Over a decade," Leo corrected me.

"And then Margot gets in touch…" I inferred.

"We hadn't talked in years—I think my dad found out

she paid for my college, and it caused some issues between the two of them, so she'd kept her distance." Leo set a large pot of water on the stove to boil, making sure to pour salt in and covering it before turning on the burner.

"That must have hurt—to have her kind of walk away like that. Was William your only ally?" I asked.

"Margot and her ex-husband fought like cats and dogs; they had a prenup, so I think she knew if they divorced—which they did a few years ago—then my father would be her only recourse. And my dad never found out about Uncle William's investment—it was from an angel investor. I only found out it was William after Dad died, although I certainly suspected it was him," Leo told me. "My father could be vindictive—he would have cut William out of the business and gone scorched earth if he found out."

"How does someone so vicious manage to be so successful?"

Leo laughed. "He came from money, and his family had a lot of connections—nobody could turn him down. I think he was softer when he was with my mom, but losing her made him hard. But I'm sure the shark was always inside him." Leo used a paring knife to slice an "X" at the bottom of each tomato. "It'll be easier to peel them," he explained without me having to ask.

"What did Margot tell you to convince you to come back home? What made you want to leave everything behind?" I took back my seat at the counter, watching Leo finish up with the tomatoes and set them next to the pot of water, which wasn't quite boiling yet.

He leaned against the counter, facing me, looking a little apprehensive. "I'm sure there was a part of me that wanted to see if he'd changed—if my success would make him love me—make him proud of me…" Leo trailed off, formulating how to say what came next. "But I think I also kind of wanted a fresh start, and it was a convenient excuse." He sighed. "Not so selfless…"

"It's not like you had anyone else looking out for you," I defended him. "What were you running away from?" I read between the lines.

Leo gave a humorless laugh, having been caught. "I was a bit bored with my work—I had a string of asshole startup CEOs, and was kind of over it at the time. And there was other stuff—a bad break up… I just needed an out."

I wanted to ask him more about the break up and "other stuff" but decided not to push my luck since he had already been so open about everything else. "Were you worried about what kind of reception you'd get?" I asked instead.

Leo shrugged. "I mean, Dad immediately accused me of only coming back to be reinstated in the will."

"And what did you say to that?" I laughed.

"I told him I wasn't expecting him to do anything of the sort, but that I wanted to try to get to know him if he really was short on time. I had my own money; I didn't need his. That shut him up real quick—I don't think he was anticipating it. Rendering him speechless for once was a nice surprise."

Leo seemed to recall the memory fondly, but it hurt my heart to think that his own father assumed Leo had only ever been interested in his money. But then again, money can easily corrupt people. Perhaps George West was just shrewd after a lifetime of feeling taken advantage of? Or maybe he was an asshole. He could have been both.

"Once he realized I planned on sticking around for a while, he opened up a little bit. Enough for me to realize it was probably a good thing that I had kept my distance, but I'd wanted to know him my whole life, and our time was limited, so I focused on making sure that he left this world with dignity. I thought I'd done that, but now I'm not so sure." Leo gently dropped the scored tomatoes into the boiling water.

"What kind of cancer was it?"

"Pancreatic—absolutely cruel, and there's barely any chance of survival. From the moment he was diagnosed, he knew…" Leo rinsed the plastic bowl and filled it half full with ice, then more water, before grabbing a second bowl from a lower cabinet.

"So you were here, helping him—"

"I mostly kept him company; he was pretty weak from the chemo, before he stopped treatment, and was just bored."

"Was Margot here a lot?" I assumed she would have been, given how hard she'd told me she'd fought to get Leo back home…although Leo's account didn't sound like it had taken much convincing. But every story has two sides, and the truth usually lies somewhere in the middle.

"She had a hard time seeing Dad like that. I think he'd always been her protector growing up, and she couldn't deal with all of it. And she'd only gotten divorced a couple years prior and was still rebuilding from that—it really shook her. Despite how much she fought with Uncle Ted, I don't think she ever thought he'd actually trade her in for a younger model, but she was wrong," Leo admitted.

"Who else was around at the time?" I was trying to piece together who would have had access to George West, and motive enough to smother him.

"Val and Carl have worked for the family for decades—Val was here every day back then; after Dad died, she asked if she could reduce her hours to one day a week because she wanted to take care of her grandkids. And Uncle William would be here more often than not—Dad insisted on staying up to date with all his business ventures and hated being on calls nonstop, so he preferred getting debriefed in person by William."

"Were you the only person taking care of your dad?" I couldn't picture Leo doing all the hard stuff that came with end-of-life care.

"We had two nurses. Julie was the main nurse, and Becky worked weekends and was backup for Julie if she was out. They were technically on call 24/7, but they'd go home at night, and I'd call them to come back if something came up that was beyond my capabilities. I only had to call them a couple times though—Dad's meds left him so tired, he slept through a lot of the day and night."

"What were they like with him?" I wanted to get a better sense of the relationship George had with his caregivers.

"Becky was timid but tough—she didn't say much, just did her work and went home. Julie was here much more often, and she had an antagonistic but playful rapport with Dad. He didn't like that he had to rely on her so much, and she didn't like that he made things difficult. But I think they both felt bad for each other in a weird way…they could commiserate." Leo used a slotted spoon to pull the tomatoes out of the boiling water and submerge them in the ice bath he'd created.

"What do you remember about the last day?" I asked softly.

Leo blew out a large breath. "It was such a blur…" He struggled to wade through specific memories while he began to peel the skin from the tomatoes.

"The morning was typical. I brought Dad coffee and helped him with his crossword puzzle. Uncle William arrived mid-morning, and I left them alone to go over their business stuff—they never asked me to leave, but I felt awkward staying. It was nice outside that day, so I ate lunch on the patio and read for a while—until Julie came out and said that she'd found Dad and that he was unresponsive." Leo paused, leaning the edge of his palms against the counter, trying not to get the tomato juice everywhere.

"It's okay, take your time," I encouraged him when he didn't continue for a moment.

"He had a DNR order in place—so once he was gone—he was gone," Leo said, staring at the counter. "I was just kind of in shock. I didn't really get to say goodbye—not like a proper goodbye. Julie took care of everything. She declared the death and arranged for transportation of his body. She was technically a hospice nurse, so she knew what to do, I guess. Someone called William and Margot—probably Julie—and they took over the funeral planning. I was like a zombie for days. I didn't cry. I didn't eat. I couldn't sleep. I couldn't feel...anything."

"Is that when the insomnia started?" I wondered aloud.

"No, it started as soon as I got back here. I didn't realize how much suppressed trauma I had from growing up in this house, and I think I was worried something would happen to him at night. The anxiety just kept me up, and then after he was gone...I don't know...maybe it's just habit at this point. Sometimes I still think I can hear his heart monitor at night." Leo looked up at me, his face pale. "You probably think I'm crazy."

"No—you're still grieving—there's no right way to do it." I reached across the counter and squeezed his hand. He squeezed back before releasing me to return to his cooking prep.

"You want to know the funniest part…?" Leo's sarcasm was evident.

I waited for him to continue.

"He'd never disinherited me." Leo laughed to himself. "His lawyer said the last time he'd changed his will was when my mom died. He left it all to me, with the stipulation that I'd make sure Margot was taken care of, and William became majority partner in all of their shared businesses, going from 49% stakeholder to 51%. That's it."

"Why do you think he told you he cut you out?"

"Maybe a test?" Leo guessed. "I was a kid—but I wouldn't put it past him. I'm sure I wasn't the best son growing up, but he was all I had left. I felt so betrayed when I left for college, and it turns out it had all been a joke to him."

"What did Margot say?"

Leo shook his head. "She was just as shocked as I was—couldn't believe he would do something like that to his own son. And it's not like he'd changed his mind when I came back to care for him—he'd never touched the thing."

Having strained the tomato chunks through a sieve to keep the seeds from the pulp, Leo set the bowl aside and began to chop some cloves of garlic on a cutting board.

"Earlier, you said you had some theories. Who do you think did it?" I inquired bluntly.

"It's not that simple. I think plenty of people over the years would have wanted to kill the old man, but whoever did it would have needed not just a motive, but also means and access." Leo's tone was methodical—he was disassociating again.

"Suffocating someone with a pillow, even if they are completely incapacitated, can take a good five minutes. This wasn't a crime of opportunity—it was premeditated, and it was personal. To stand there for five minutes and smother him…" Leo dropped his knife on the cutting board, the thoughts becoming too intrusive for him to focus on such a delicate and dangerous task at the same time.

"So let's run through your list of suspects," I proposed. "I suppose we can rule you out, because if you had done it, you never would have proceeded with all the private autopsies—"

"Or gone to the police," Leo added.

"You went to the police?" I was surprised he was only mentioning it now.

"That's where I was for most of the day yesterday. They didn't take too kindly to me showing up and trying to reopen what they'd ruled an open and closed case—an easy natural death. A couple of the pathologists did warn me, to be fair." Leo resumed mincing the garlic.

"Warned you about what?"

"Said the police didn't like it when civilians second-guessed their work. The last one also said that the evidence she discovered looks like suffocation when it's all put together, but individually, she understood why they gave the original cause of death." Leo scraped the garlic into a pan, poured a fair amount of expensive-looking olive oil in after it, and then turned the burner back on.

"She said his eyes were bloodshot, which is typical of suffocation, but his meds made his eyes bloodshot too—and everyone knew that; he hated it and complained about it to anyone who visited. His appearance was important to him— that's why he refused to go into the office or do video calls at the end.

"The first pathologist said they only found the fibers in his mouth because they were looking for them, the second also found what they call petechial hemorrhages on his lungs—the coroner didn't open him up because they had no reason to before, so they wouldn't have seen it. There were no signs of struggle, which meant he was likely sedated, but that wasn't unusual for him. But all of those things added up. I just wish the police would have listened to me." Leo sighed.

"What exactly did they say?" I ventured.

"That they'd look into it." Leo rolled his eyes. "They had some desk jockey take my information. I could tell they won't take it seriously. If I don't figure this out myself, his killer will remain free."

"I'll do whatever I can to help you," I promised him.

Leo gave a gentle nod of appreciation.

"Is that why the solarium is off-limits?" I asked, suddenly realizing, at the thought of the police, that maybe it wasn't grief alone that kept that door locked.

"Yeah, but a fat lot of good that did." He grimaced. "I still have no idea how it got open that day, but since it wasn't you, I have to assume that the crime scene has been contaminated."

"You think the killer came back?" I asked, brows raised. "Why?"

"No idea." Leo shrugged. "Maybe if we can figure it out, it will give us a clue as to who they are."

"So William was the last visitor, and then Nurse Julie found him," I repeated. "Could someone have snuck into the solarium from outside? I know you've got the ancient security system, but I haven't seen any cameras on the property."

"I suppose someone could have. We didn't keep the solarium locked during the day; if it was nice out, like that day, Dad liked the fresh air." Leo began adding all sorts of spices and bits to the pan with the olive oil and garlic, using a flat wooden spoon to move everything around to keep it from burning.

"But like you said, this was too personal, and would have taken too long. It's unlikely to be an outsider—or if it was, they would have been assisted by someone inside."

"Exactly." Leo slowly began to add the tomato pulp into the pan. "I'll look into a security system though, now that you mention it."

"So who does that leave us with? Where was everyone that day, other than William and the nurse?" I returned to our list of suspects.

"Margot was a few towns over, helping with some charity event." Leo continued to stir the sauce, adding more spices every now and then.

"But she was staying in the back cottage at the time?" I clarified.

"Yes; she's been living there for at least three years."

"And what about motive?"

"I mean, you could argue money for everyone on our short list." Leo frowned. "But she's got a black AmEx without a limit that my father paid off every month without asking questions, and I do the same. She wants for nothing."

"Do you know where William was before and after his visit?" I asked.

"Probably the office; I don't know if they'd have records—maybe GPS if his phone was tracking his location as he drove?" Leo suggested.

I was impressed with Leo; he'd clearly given this a lot of thought.

"He majorly benefited from your father's will—getting to take over the businesses." I liked William, but he had both means and motive. "And you said it yourself that he was here all the time—he'd know everyone's habits and schedules. He was the last person to—"

"I know!" Leo snapped quietly. "I just—in my gut, I don't think he did it. He's been more of a father to me than my actual father. I just don't think he has it in him. And my dad was dying anyway—why the rush? They didn't have any major deals or issues at the companies around the time Dad died. It just doesn't make any sense."

I put my hands up defensively. "We're just talking through the facts. I'm not accusing anyone."

"Sorry..." Leo exhaled.

"It's okay," I consoled him. "This is...a lot."

Leo covered the simmering saucepan with a lid, then returned to the counter, facing me. "Who's next?" he said, ready to continue.

"You mentioned Val and Carl. How long have they worked for your family?"

"Val's had to have been here for over thirty years; she practically raised me. I know she was here before my parents were married. Like I said, she was full-time up until Dad died. And for as much of an asshole as he could be, he was actually pretty generous with his staff: both Val and Carl."

"Generous how?" I was curious.

Leo pulled the pasta dough from the plastic wrap and began to flatten it with a rolling pin after sprinkling some flour on the counter. "Gave them whatever time off they needed for family stuff and holidays, always gave large holiday bonuses. Growing up, I was always jealous because I thought he was nicer to them than he was to me.

"I don't see a motive for either of them, regardless of access...unless there were some deep-seated feelings of resentment built up over the years or something?" Leo seemed to be grasping at straws. "There was just a camaraderie he had with both of them; they're both hardworking, discreet, and loyal—that's all my dad ever wanted from them."

"We can't exactly rule them out without talking to them. But I agree, they seem less likely."

"So who does that leave?" Leo asked, as he started cutting the flattened dough into long strips, winding every couple strips together into a small twisted ball, then moving on to the next.

"The nurses."

"Right." Leo contemplated them for a few moments. "I suppose they had just as much access as me. Becky, the backup nurse, I'd put her on the bottom of the list with Val and Carl because she wasn't around as much, and wasn't there that day, that I know of. But I suppose we'll have to confirm with her to rule her out as well."

I watched Leo's eyes darting back and forth, not focusing on the pasta in front of him, but rather, trying to review what he knew of the other nurse.

"I have no idea why Julie would have done it." Leo sounded perplexed. "I knew her a little less than a year; she started right before I came home, when Dad was placed in palliative care here."

I could sense there was something Leo was holding back. "What is it?"

Leo's shoulders slumped. "She was here for a year, and she took care of him almost every day, and I feel like I don't know anything about her—I never bothered to ask."

He felt guilty.

"I think that was understandable, considering everything

that was going on."

"I guess—I just…" Leo paused. "You're right."

"William and Julie are still at the top of the list for me," I decided. "Do you have any contact information for Julie?"

"I'm not sure; I'll have to check."

"What do you want to do about your uncle?" I asked gently.

"Nothing yet," Leo said quickly. "I want to talk to Julie first."

I nodded in understanding.

"I don't think I can talk about this anymore tonight." Leo's face was drawn.

"Okay." I smiled softly.

We didn't say much else while Leo finished making dinner. The joy he'd felt at using his new kitchen for the first time seemed to have evaporated. But he appeared more resolute than he had at the beginning of the evening.

He had a mission now.

And I had the best bowl of pasta I'd ever eaten in my entire life…which I made the mistake of letting Leo know.

His ego had never been so out of control.

CHAPTER 7

THE DIARY

I had trouble sleeping the night Leo shared everything about his father's death with me.

I would have thought the delicious food would have put me right to sleep, but I couldn't turn my mind off. There was something he'd said that didn't feel right, but I couldn't put my finger on what it was. It would torture me for days to come.

It didn't help that I could hear him below, puttering around the kitchen, cleaning up the mess from dinner, which I had offered to do myself, but he had vehemently refused. I was also pretty sure he was reorganizing the cabinets to his preferences.

When I finally drifted off into some kind of light sleep, after the regular 2:13 a.m. thump from the attic, I was plagued by scratching and shuffling noises coming from the walls. I was positive it wasn't from an animal, but if not an animal, I had no idea what could have caused it.

The next morning, I wasn't even sure if it had really happened, or if it had merely been a waking dream. I did, however, find it odd that my cell phone had moved clear across the room while I slept. I was sure I had set it on the nightstand before bed, and it was on the floor, next to the window, when I awoke. Whether I had moved it, or someone else had, the fact that it wasn't where I thought I'd left it unnerved me.

Over the weekend, similar occurrences happened both while I was sleeping and during the day, when I had been nowhere near the pink room. Random bits would move around my room, leaving me questioning my sanity.

I was positively spooked.

When I brought it up to Leo over dinner on Sunday night, he was just as perplexed. "You're sure it wasn't you?"

"If it was, I have no memory of doing any of it," I assured him.

He pursed his lips, unsure of what to make of the phenomenon. "Don't say it," he warned me.

"What?"

Leo glared.

Ghosts.

Hauntings.

He didn't like the idea of any of it. Neither did I, but at least it would have explained what was going on. I didn't like the idea of being mad, myself.

"I've been meaning to ask," Leo began, "when they start the flooring tomorrow, if you want, you can sleep in my room for a few days."

"Oh." I managed. "Thank you." The offer was unexpected, but solved a problem that had been nagging at me for a while. "Are you sure?"

"If you don't mind, I don't—it's not like I use it overnight." He gave a mirthless laugh.

"When *do* you sleep?" I asked. I only understood the broad strokes of insomnia.

"I'll fall asleep on the couch most nights, at some point. Occasionally, if I'm overly tired, I'll nap during the day." He sipped his coffee.

"Have you seen anyone about it?" I might have been overstepping, but Leo had been opening up so much more, I thought it was worth a chance.

"Sure—I've got pills. I just hate taking them; they make me feel like a zombie the next day, and sometimes, if they don't work, it puts me in this awful headspace while my brain fights the drugs to stay awake. I'll feel agitated—anxious for hours; hyperaware of my surroundings." Leo shook his head, as if he was trying to shake the memories away. "I didn't take them for long," he confessed.

"I'm sorry."

Leo looked up at me, over his coffee, a small smile tugging at his lips. "It's okay—it hasn't been as bad recently…and the new couch is so much more comfortable than the old one."

I returned his smile.

That evening, Leo showed me into his room for the first time.

He had previously explained that it used to be his father's study. He had converted it into a bedroom, so he could be close to the solarium at night, if he was needed. His explanation made the dark paneling along the walls make sense. I could easily see the large wood desk from the library in the middle of the room, with George West seated behind it, angrily telling off investors.

The entire right-hand wall was lined with bookshelves. Opposite, on the left side, Leo's bed was centered on the wall. Leo explained that the door on the right of his bed led to the bathroom, which was also accessible through the solarium.

"I won't go in there," I said immediately. I had learned my lesson.

"I know," he replied confidently.

His bed was as dark and moody as the rest of the room, with charcoal linen sheets and a black duvet of the same material. But it looked so much cozier than the bed in the pink room. I had to resist the urge to dive in and make myself comfortable.

Along the wall between the main door and the bookshelves was a clothing rack, where a few suit coats hung. A thick chest of drawers stood next to it, where I assumed Leo kept the rest of his clothes, since the study didn't have a proper closet.

Heavy dark-blue velvet curtains lined the entirety of the wall facing out to the backyard. I wondered when they had last been opened. Maybe never.

I knew from having seen it from the backyard that they concealed a window seat that matched the one in the library.

"I'll be in the living room if you need anything; I'll be quiet—I know how sound can travel in this old house," he joked awkwardly before taking his leave, closing the door gently behind him.

Sitting down on Leo's bed, I realized it was as comfortable as I had imagined. I took time to let my eyes wander around the room. I was still touched by the trust he had placed in me, to allow me into his personal space…his sanctuary. I resolved not to touch a single thing, so as not to violate that trust.

Our bond had definitely grown in the weeks I'd been staying at the house, but there were still moments it felt tenuous. I didn't want to do anything to jeopardize my friendship with Leo. Project aside, I felt we had grown to rely on each other in small ways, and I would have been devastated to lose that.

Leo's bedroom was tastefully appointed. I did want to brighten it up a bit, but it suited his state of mind, and it was *his*—perhaps the only part of that house that he could claim as solely his own. While it was minimalistic, the masculine elements felt right for the space…they felt right for him.

Being surrounded by his musky scent, in his bed, albeit alone, I had to finally admit defeat. I had feelings for Leo beyond a friendship. I'd been pulled to him since the beginning, and I thought he must have been drawn to me in some kind of way as well, or he never would have taken a chance on me like he had.

When I thought of Leo, he made me feel warm. I liked being around him. I loved the way we made each other laugh. I smiled as I realized I could bring out a lightness in him that I hadn't seen anyone else capable of. It made me feel special.

The warmth spread.

I was in trouble. He was still my boss.

And I wasn't sure what to do about any of it.

Waking up in Leo's room the first morning almost felt like a dream. His bed was beyond cozy, and even though he wasn't in the room with me, it felt like he was all around me, like he had held me in his arms all night. I hadn't slept so well in ages. I didn't want to get up.

But alas, duty called, and I knew a fresh cup of coffee and Leo himself awaited me in the kitchen.

"I can't find her anywhere," Leo said dejectedly as he slid my steaming mug across the counter.

I watched him as he poured more coffee into his own mug, then took a seat next to me at the counter. His thigh touched mine, sending a zing of electricity up my spine. I was surprised when he made no attempt to sever the connection.

"Who?" I was still groggy from finally receiving the deep sleep I had so desperately needed.

"Julie—the nurse," Leo clarified. "Did you sleep okay?" His brow furrowed as he got a good look at me.

"Yeah. Too well, actually." I chuckled, trying to ignore the heat of his thigh against mine.

Leo raised a brow, confused by my humor.

"Your mattress was so much more comfortable than the one in the pink room," I told him. "And I think—" I paused, unsure if I wanted to say what came next, but I did anyway. "I think I felt a lot safer knowing you were right outside," I admitted.

Leo paused, taking in what I'd said. "I didn't realize you felt unsafe upstairs." He seemed upset.

"Not unsafe exactly—just on edge, I guess." I didn't quite know how to put to words the uncomfortable feeling that enveloped me, in the dark, alone, in the pink room, with all the odd noises and goings on—it had become oppressive.

"I'm sorry." Leo's brow furrowed, perhaps feeling responsible.

He wasn't.

"Don't worry about it." I waved him off. "What were you saying about Julie?"

"Margot was useless—she's terrible with names and faces. But what's worse is that I can't find a single trace of her online—and I'm good at tracking this kind of stuff. It's like she never existed."

"How did you find her? Through a referral? Or an agency?" I asked, unsure of how someone finds an at-home hospice nurse.

"I'll have to call Dad's doctor and see if they know—she was hired before I came back. Otherwise I know a PI that's helped me before," Leo threw out casually.

"You just happen to know a private investigator?" I narrowly avoided choking on my coffee.

"Back when I was consulting—sometimes we'd have to research competitors, fraudulent business claims, or track down leaks on IP."

"IP?" I'd heard the term before, but couldn't remember what it stood for.

"Intellectual property—usually proprietary information that made the startup special or unique in the marketplace. Often, startups are taken advantage of, if the people running things aren't business savvy enough—trusting the wrong people." He finished his coffee and got up to rinse the mug. "They usually can't afford physical or cyber security measures either."

"Huh." I looked down at my half full mug, again trying to think about anything other than Leo's thighs.

"Can you handle the flooring guys solo so I can try to

track down our missing nurse?" Leo asked.

"Sure. Danny will be here any minute, and he'll keep everyone in check." I laughed, thinking of Danny's already red face getting redder if the new contractors stepped out of line.

"I'm going to change quick," Leo told me. I was perplexed for a moment, before I realized he was telling me because we were effectively sharing the same room now.

I felt bad, thinking that because I had invaded his space, he hadn't been able to wear fresh clothes. I had to remind myself that he had invited me to stay in his room, and he wouldn't have done so if he wasn't okay with it.

A few minutes later, Leo was at the door putting his coat on.

"Be safe." I leaned against the railing of the main staircase, feeling a strange desire to remind him to be cautious—something about the situation just felt off.

"I'll keep you posted." He reached out and squeezed my hand. The gesture, having been initiated by him, flared the warmth brewing inside of me.

"Bye," I sighed as he released me, the loss of his warmth immediate. Maybe my feelings weren't so one-sided?

Leo almost ran into Danny on his way out.

"Sorry, sir." Danny bristled.

"Entirely my fault." Leo chuckled, giving Danny half a wave before heading for his car.

"You ready for some new floors?" Danny's smile

brightened the room and my mood.

The flooring contractors arrived shortly after Danny and got to work right away stripping the disgusting and decrepit shag carpeting from the second floor. Painstakingly removing every single staple and finishing nail that had kept the carpet in place for decades took us the entire rest of the day.

While they were busy upstairs, I decided to start the incredibly laborious task of reorganizing and cataloging the library. Leo and I had been talking about it for weeks and putting it off for just as long, knowing how manual and intensive it would be.

But at least in that time we had come up with a game plan, and Leo had decided how he wanted everything arranged. So what was left was to remove all the books from their shelves, organize, alphabetize, itemize, and return them to their rightful places, in some sort of order that made sense to Leo, which was all that mattered to me.

It was almost dark out when the last of the crew left and Leo returned home, takeout in hand.

"Already sick of cooking?" I joked, secretly appreciative I wouldn't have to wait a moment longer to eat, as I'd forgotten about lunch, having been buried beneath stacks of ancient encyclopedias and long-outdated textbooks on every kind of subject matter under the sun.

"Never." Leo shook his head, smiling.

"Any luck?" I hedged.

"Doctor's office gave me the name of an agency, but

they wouldn't release any personal information." Leo began unpacking the bag, laying out the food and utensils neatly across the counter. "I reached out to my friend; he's going to help me look into it and agreed it's weird she's not online anywhere."

"I'm glad you have help," I sympathized.

"What did you get up to today?" Leo changed the subject.

"Flooring guys are almost done pulling tacks out of the second floor"—I paused, unsure of how he would react to the next part— "and I started organizing the library."

Leo raised a brow. "Did you?"

"I hope you don't mind—it felt weird lording over a bunch of grown men picking at tacks and nails one at a time upstairs," I joked.

"How far did you get?"

"Not far." I laughed. "But I've been entering everything into a spreadsheet as I go, so you have a full catalog."

Leo nodded in approval, taking a bite of his food.

The rest of the week went by much the same. Leo went out chasing down leads and working with his "PI friend," who didn't seem to have a name, while I buried myself in books, and the men slowly refinished the flooring upstairs. By Thursday, the seal had been put over the newly sanded and stained hardwoods and was left to cure overnight. Danny was right, his friend did good work. They left with a promise to be back in a couple weeks, after Thanksgiving, to start working on the main floor.

"You sure you want to move back upstairs?" Leo asked suspiciously over coffee on Friday morning.

I hesitated, causing his eyes to narrow. I knew whatever excuse I gave, he'd never accept it now. So I merely shrugged. "I'll be fine," I lied.

The truth was that for as much as I wanted to stay in his room, I was also aware I wanted it *too much*. What was worse was that I wanted him in there with me. I was fighting an internal battle, and being in that room made it so much more difficult to ignore my feelings and pretend that I felt nothing when I was around him.

How do you ignore your heart skipping a beat every time someone enters a room, or smiles at you, or lets their gaze linger a moment too long, leaving you wondering if you've imagined their interest or willed it into being?

Of course I didn't want to banish myself back up to the haunted pink room, as far from Leo as I could get, but if I didn't, I wasn't sure what would happen.

"Won't the fumes bother you?" Leo tried.

I shook my head. "They aired everything out yesterday; it's safe."

Leo snorted a laugh at the word "safe," implying that the term was relative. He wasn't wrong.

"I'll order new mattresses for the rooms upstairs—the same one I have down here," he offered.

I shrugged again. "If you want."

Leo's brow furrowed, confused by my indifference.

"That would be nice," I corrected myself.

Leo relaxed, having been given permission to help. "Do you plan on redecorating the rooms now that the floors are finished?" he asked. We'd been gathering items slowly as we visited antique stores in the area, scoured online for special vintage pieces, and kept tabs on what would go where inside the house.

I nodded emphatically. "But I need to finish the library first." I took a sip of my coffee. "I'd have a hard time focusing on the rooms if I left it in chaos."

"I'll help if I can," Leo told me, "but Val and Carl will both be here today—I was hoping to talk to them—see if they have any insight about Dad."

"Good—maybe they know something about Julie too. Don't worry about the library; I've got it under control."

After coffee, we went our separate ways, and once again, I lost time as I sorted through the never-ending stacks of books waiting for me in the organized chaos of the library.

It wasn't long after I started sorting through the books that I came upon a small leather-bound journal that had been slipped between the pages of an old encyclopedia from the seventies.

Skimming the first few pages of old paper, imprints still visible from the blue ballpoint pen, it became apparent that the journal had once belonged to Christine West, Leo's mother.

I closed the journal, not feeling right about reading it without him.

Journal in hand, I went out to the kitchen, looking for Leo, calling out for him, but he wasn't on the main floor.

"He left about twenty minutes ago." Val poked her head out from the storage room behind the kitchen. "Did you need help with something?"

I'd had minimal interaction with Val since starting the project and, curiously, even less after I'd moved in. I wasn't sure if she was just intent on keeping to herself, or if she was actively avoiding me. But the few times we had spoken, she'd seemed nice enough; she just didn't like to waste time talking, preferring to keep herself busy with work.

I looked down at the journal, then back up at Val. "Did he say when he'd be back?" I asked.

Val shook her head. A single strand of silver hair escaped from her tight braid, but she quickly tucked it behind her ear.

"Thanks," I replied, then made my way back into the library. I thought about texting Leo, but he was probably driving, and if he wasn't, he'd left to meet someone, still on the hunt for Nurse Julie.

Feeling guilty but hoping Leo wouldn't be upset, I made the decision to read through the journal. Margot had always been so brief about what had happened to Christine, and nobody else would even say her name—Leo himself became anxious at the mention of his mother. And selfishly, I think part of me knew there was a chance that once I turned the journal over to Leo, I'd never get the opportunity to look through it again.

I felt like a bad person—like a bad friend—but I read the journal anyway.

I was simply too curious.

And it was a good thing, in this case.

The journal seemed to have been written right around the time of Christine's death. My eyes flew through the pages, desperate to find some insight into what had happened to the woman.

The earlier entries started innocently enough. She was happy with George but felt he spent too much time at work, and she felt his absence keenly. She thought he was missing Leo's childhood, and it broke her heart.

Most entries mentioned Leo, a toddler at the time, in some capacity. Christine was absolutely in love with her baby. The more I read, the more I felt confused about why she had taken her own life. The way she spoke about Leo and her desire to watch him grow up didn't read as someone who was suicidal, or depressed—it was the opposite.

I did have to consider that people see their own lives differently than others, and she might not have been telling the whole truth, even in her personal diary. Maybe it had been an exercise from a therapist, or she'd known George was reading it, so she'd written what they'd wanted to hear? But if that wasn't the case, if this record was simply for Christine and Christine alone, then surely she wouldn't have ended her life unless something catastrophic had happened.

I didn't see any underlining or subtextual clues that would lead me to believe that this woman would die at her own hand within months of writing such sweet words about how quickly Leo was growing up and how she couldn't wait to see the man he would become. She'd had no idea that wouldn't happen.

But about halfway through the journal, there was a tonal shift. Christine had discovered something, and whatever it was, she wasn't comfortable spelling it out precisely on the pages…maybe she was worried someone was reading what she wrote.

Throughout the diary, she referred to someone, who seemed to be a close friend, using an odd symbol that looked like four narrow, closely spaced capital "X's" next to each other: XXXX Whoever they were, they were a voice of reason, a shoulder to cry on, and very much a confidante.

The first entry I flagged started with '*XXXX can't be trusted. If George found out what they did, he'd kill them, and Leo would lose his father.*'

A few days later, Christine wrote, '*Can't stop thinking about XXXX Poor Thomas and Mary. They didn't deserve what happened to them. I'm trying to see if George knows anyone at the police station. If I can turn in XXXX before George finds out and tries to handle it himself, maybe I can make this right.*'

But then things took a turn, and the last entry read, '*I*

think XXX knows something is wrong. They always know when I'm not telling the truth. They can tell something is bothering me. I'm scared for Leo. I've started hiding this diary around the house. If XXX found it, I'm done for.'

My heart beat loudly in my chest as I closed the journal. Christine's fear was so palpable. I didn't think she'd killed herself. I was almost positive someone had pushed her off the seaside cliff.

Whoever XXX was, it sounded like they not only had played a role in Christine's murder, but that they had done something to the Thomas and Mary she mentioned. I didn't know who they were, but clearly they were people who had meant a great deal to George, enough that Christine thought he would risk his own freedom for revenge.

I called Leo, but it went straight to voicemail.

His phone was off.

Where was he?

It was getting dark out, and he'd been gone for hours.

Holding the journal tightly, I ventured out of the library, back into the living room. "Val?" I called, but nobody responded. It would have been unlike her to stay on that late anyway. But if Val was gone, that meant I was alone in the house.

Feeling suddenly exposed, as if the house knew I was aware of some long-forgotten secrets that nobody was meant to discover, I double-checked that the front door was locked before sprinting up to the pink room and locking myself inside.

I texted Leo, telling him I was worried about him and that I needed to talk to him. I hoped that when he turned his phone on again, he'd see the text and get ahold of me.

Sitting in the room by myself, every noise, every shadow, every movement out of the corner of my eye unnerved me. Even with the new sheets, rearranged floor plan, and different smell, thanks to the newly sealed flooring, the room still felt off. But I didn't know where else to go.

Well, there was one other place, but if Leo found me in his room uninvited, even if I felt safer there…I didn't want another reaction like what had happened when he'd discovered me in the solarium. It wasn't worth the potential respite.

I turned off the lights, thinking that maybe if I couldn't see anything, it would calm my nerves. And perhaps it worked a little too well. Coming down from the adrenaline, I fell fast asleep, clutching the journal to my chest.

CHAPTER 8

SHADOWS

I awoke with a start; it was still dark outside.

Briefly, I wondered if the regular 2:13 a.m. thump had jostled me from sleep, or perhaps Leo had finally returned home and forgotten that any noise he made in the kitchen echoed throughout the house like a cavern.

But then I heard what had pulled me from slumber. The scraping noises had returned, and they were coming from the corner of the room where a dark shadow loomed. Feeling my heart racing, I panicked, trying to figure out what to do.

I could run.

I could yell.

I could throw something at the shadow.

I ran through a list of items before realizing that something was missing.

The journal.

I knew I'd gone to sleep with it, but it was gone.

I patted around the bed, but there was nothing.

It could have fallen on the ground, but if a small scratching noise had woken me up, I assumed the thud of the journal on the hardwood would have as well.

The scratching continued, and I began to feel lightheaded as hyperventilation sunk in.

So I made the choice to run.

And I ran fast.

Skittering down the stairs, I almost ran straight into Leo, who was just as alarmed with my sudden appearance as I was to see him.

"Where were you!?" I cried; the terror of the shadow figure in the corner was still seeping into me.

"Whoa—slow down—what happened?"

"There was someone—something in my room." I shuddered.

Leo's face paled.

"It's okay—I'll check it out." He darted into the kitchen and grabbed a large knife from the butcher block. "You want to stay down here?" he asked, trying to stay calm, despite the tremble to his voice.

"Alone!?" I yelped.

"Okay-okay." He held my forearm, trying to reason with

me. "Stay behind me—no sudden movements."

Slowly, we made our way up the stairs, turning on every single light in our wake. If there really was a person up there, the house was old enough, we would hear them if they tried to go down the back stairs, and they would have to pass us if they tried to descend the front staircase.

"Hello? Anyone there?" Leo called out.

Nobody answered except my heavy breathing behind him.

Leo kicked the door to the pink room open and darted inside to switch on the light.

The room was empty.

My eyes snapped to the floor as I rounded the bed.

The journal was really gone.

I wondered if I'd imagined all of it. I opened my mouth to tell Leo what I'd discovered, but found that the words wouldn't come out.

I needed to find that journal. He'd never believe me without it. It was all too outlandish, and terribly convenient.

"Where did you see them?" Leo asked.

I pointed to the far corner, next to the window. "It was a big shadow—it was making a scraping sound. I know I sound crazy." I could feel the tears welling up in my eyes.

"Hey." He grabbed my hand, squeezing it. "It's okay. Whatever you saw, I believe you."

I looked down at the floor, unable to meet his gaze. I felt like I was going insane.

"Let's check the other rooms just to be safe," he suggested.

One by one, we looked around the empty rooms and found nothing.

"I tried to call you," I sniffled.

We walked back down the main stairs. Leo kept my hand firmly in his. The connection helped more than he knew.

"When?" His brow furrowed as he dug his phone out of his pocket, finally letting my hand drop as he tried to turn it on. "Shit—the battery died." He looked up at me apologetically. "I'm so sorry, Pen."

"It's not your fault." I swallowed the lump in my throat.

"I didn't know." He shook his head, plugging it into a charger on the kitchen island. "Are you okay?" He rubbed his hand up and down my arm.

I nodded, not trusting my voice to reply.

"I got home a little later than usual, and I found you asleep upstairs. I didn't want to wake you up."

I wanted to ask him if he remembered if I had been holding anything when he came up to check on me, but without the evidence, it was pointless. I shoved the urge aside.

"Did you eat dinner? I brought you sushi; it's in the fridge." He pointed behind him.

"I didn't eat." I shook my head.

"Go sit down in the living room, I'll bring it over. And Pen?"

I turned back toward him.

"Breathe. You're okay." He smiled softly.

I let out a deep exhale, already feeling so much better that he was here.

I wasn't alone.

I hadn't been alone in that room either.

The shadow was gone…but so was the journal…

Something warm moved beneath me, bringing me to a somewhat conscious state. My sleepy gaze met Leo's. I had fallen asleep on him, in the living room.

"What time is it?" I grumbled.

"Early enough—you want some coffee?" Leo's husky morning voice was a rare treat.

I nodded, leaning back into the sofa, running my hands over my face.

"Sorry," I said without thinking.

"Why?" Leo slowly stood from the couch—had he slept too?

"For falling asleep on you—how embarrassing." I chuckled.

"So embarrassing." He laughed with me, simultaneously dismissing my concerns.

"I need to change," I thought aloud. I was still wearing jeans and a blazer from the day before.

"Coffee will be ready in five," Leo replied.

In the gray morning light, the upstairs didn't look as scary as the night before. It didn't hurt that Leo had left all the lights on overnight. I turned them off one by one as I walked through the second floor, also searching for the lost journal. I really was beginning to wonder if I'd made up the entire thing.

I spent most of the day nervously searching the rest of the house with no luck, while Leo watched me from afar, unaware of what I was doing, and while he seemed to be concerned with my state of mind, he let me proceed without hindering my efforts.

I turned up absolutely nothing.

By the time a storm rolled in, late afternoon, the house had begun to get dark, and I no longer felt safe wandering around alone, so I made my way back to the living room, where Leo had been reading most of the day, when he wasn't tending to a roast he'd been watching scrupulously in the slow cooker.

Sheets of rain and wind pelted the wall of windows in the living room, startling me more than once before Leo relented and decided to close the curtains. We had an arrangement that they would remain open during daylight, but since the storm had brought twilight early, I didn't argue with him. But we could still see the flashes of lighting through the transom windows above the larger windows, which weren't covered by curtains, as well as through some of the frosted glass windows around the front door.

Over a glass of wine, and Leo's delicious dinner, he could sense that something was still amiss. "You sure you're alright?"

"It's the storm—my nerves are shot." I gave him a half-truth. And right on cue, thunder rumbled across the sky, angrily agreeing with my assessment.

"I'm worried about you," he admitted, "You can tell me what's going on."

Just as he'd told me that night in the library, when he'd confessed I was the only person he trusted…he could see right through me. Lying was a pointless game. But I wasn't ready to spill everything. I still held out hope I could find the journal.

"I don't think I can sleep in the pink room again." I sighed in defeat.

Leo smiled softly. "You don't have to go back up there—you can sleep in my room for as long as you want."

I hadn't expected him to put that on the table. "Really?" The thought of getting a good night's sleep in his soft, warm, comfy bed that smelled like him made my heart soar.

"Sure—after what happened last night, I don't blame you. I don't want you to feel uncomfortable here." He took another bite of his food. "You want another glass?" Leo pointed to my empty stemware.

I nodded, smiling for the first time in a while. I wasn't sure if it was the thought that I wouldn't have to be alone, in the dark, in that awful room anymore, or simply the wine, but I felt the familiar warmth tingle through me.

I think maybe Leo was feeling the wine too, because when he came back over to the couch with two more glasses for each of us, he surprised me when he said, "It's been really nice to have you around the last few weeks."

"I'm very grateful you opened your home up to me when I had nowhere else to go."

He nodded, signaling that he wasn't fishing for compliments, but appreciated them nonetheless. "It's been really hard since Dad died—honestly, since before then too…"

"You mentioned you were kind of running away from some stuff when you decided to come back to Willowbrooke." I recalled our conversation the night he had made pasta for me. Would I finally find out the truth of what he'd left behind, and why?

"I spent most of my twenties networking and building up relationships and word of mouth to find new opportunities consulting for startups," he began. "I wouldn't have said it then, but it's obvious now that I was trying to make a name for myself—trying to show my dad that I didn't need him. Trying to prove him wrong."

"How did you get into that in the first place?" I asked.

A flash of light and a huge clap of thunder temporarily prevented him from responding. The wind and rain were still wailing outside the house. I assumed being up on top of the cliff made conditions worse at Willowbrooke.

"I have a business degree and got an MBA right after. I worked at a handful of startups, trying to help with operations and finances, but I noticed a pattern that the make-or-break moment for each of them was whether or not they could scale their business. Whether the business idea was scalable, or whether management was the problem—scalability was always the core issue." He took another bite of his dinner.

"That was awfully clever of you to see so early in your career and take advantage of it to build your own brand."

"Maybe growing up around Dad and Uncle William finally rubbed off on me." He chuckled. "But the more companies I consulted for, the more I became jaded by a lot of it. So many of these startups were run by rich kids—trust fund babies who were playing around with money like it meant nothing." Leo paused.

"I was one of them once." He leaned back into the couch. "I mean, I'd like to think I wasn't a brat about it when I was younger, and I *hate* to admit that Dad pretending to disinherit me actually worked by teaching me the value of money, but it was more about how they didn't see that the decisions they made affected people who couldn't afford to just move onto the next project as easily. There were lives at stake, and they didn't care. It got harder and harder to keep going. So I was ready to figure something else out when everything changed."

Even though I had grown up in an upper-middle-class home, because of how my parents treated me, I'd always felt a drive to fend for myself. They made it clear early on, when they refused to support changing my major from architecture to interior design, that I was on my own. And as the office manager at the firm, although it was nepotism that got me the job, I barely scraped by, which they knew. But I refused to ask them for help.

I preferred to struggle instead of admit defeat. Not with them.

Leo was the same.

"And then there was Quinn…" Leo sighed heavily, then took a large pull of wine.

I waited quietly for him to continue. Seeing Leo this bare, this exposed, I knew I needed to let him speak in his own time.

"She worked at one of the startups where I was consulting. She was bright, gregarious, and we had so much in common. We were together for over two years when I proposed."

I nearly spit out the sip of wine I'd taken, but managed to swallow it instead.

"When Margot quietly reached out to me after her divorce, she took quite a liking to Quinn. They became very close, and it felt like Quinn was the daughter she'd never had. I think Quinn really helped Margot process her divorce and was a good distraction while she was picking up the pieces.

"But after a while, I could tell something had changed. And when Margot told me about Dad being sick—Quinn pushed me to go home and reconcile with him, which was weird because she knew how much I'd gone through because of him.

"After being home for a while, the veil kind of lifted, and I started to see her in a different light. She barely called, visited maybe once or twice, and only asked if things had gotten better between us. And it dawned on me that the whole time, she had only been with me for money—for status.

"I think at some point, Margot told her I'd been disinherited, and that's why she was so keen on me reconnecting with him. When I realized that, so many things started to make sense, little things that I had noticed and tried to ignore. And once I understood what I really was to her, there was no putting us back together."

"That must have been devastating," I commented delicately.

"I hadn't felt so betrayed since Dad basically told me I was on my own." Leo looked down at his wineglass while he swirled the remaining liquid. "Margot was destroyed when she found out I broke off the engagement.

"Quinn denied everything, but so much fell into place; I didn't believe her. Like she was always bringing me to these awful black-tie events under the guise of networking, but she wasn't trying to help me, she was trying to help herself. I saw her for exactly who she was, and everything she did was for her own benefit.

"Margot tried to interfere—tried to help mediate, but I was done. That trust was broken and was never going to be repaired. And what's funny is that I knew it was the right thing because when I told her we were over, I felt so much lighter. I'd never felt more free in my life. Even Dad could see that a weight had been lifted off my shoulders.

"But it wasn't until I met you that I realized how lonely I've been the past couple years." His voice was soft…yearning. "Or how nice it is to be with someone who actually cares about you with no strings attached…"

I looked up at Leo then, not realizing how close his face was to mine.

In the dim light, the shadows of insomnia gathered below his eyes were more pronounced. Leo didn't just look physically tired, he looked mentally exhausted. Grieving his father had not been kind to him; I wished there was something I could do to comfort him through his loss.

Our eyes locked for a brief moment, hazel on blue, before I involuntarily closed the gap between us.

If I thought the warmth I had felt at his fleeting touches and attention were satiating, it had nothing on the sparks that flew the moment my lips met his.

Surprised by Leo's immediate acceptance of my advances and hungry reciprocation, what started as a quick, intense, and passionate kiss turned languid, soft, and sweet. He tasted only of the wine we had imbibed, and smelled like the salty ocean air.

My senses were so completely overwhelmed. I felt lost in the moment, but never more glad to be so.

Leo and I clung to each other, desperate to get closer as the kiss deepened. His hands were firmly wrapped around me, one pressed against the base of my neck, while the other was at the small of my back. I snaked one of my arms around his torso, allowing my fingers to grip his shoulder muscles along his back; the other was pinned between us, my fingers splayed across the scruff at his jawline.

We separated briefly, both gasping for breath, before he leaned in again, powerless to stop himself, as the glass separating us from this taboo had been irrevocably shattered. I was both unable and unwilling to deny him.

His hands went to my waist, and I leaned forward, balancing precariously on one knee while I swung the other across him, allowing me to straddle him. I felt his fingers graze my stomach as he tugged at the hem of my shirt. I could feel how much he wanted me as I settled on top of him, unable to stop the rocking movement my hips made against him.

I wanted Leo with every fiber of my being, and with a couple of glasses of wine in my system, I was ready to throw all caution to the wind, jeopardizing everything I had worked so hard to achieve, just to have a taste of what life could be like with him.

I was prepared to surrender myself to the feelings that had been building for weeks, if not months, but had been suppressed so vehemently that they now crashed over me like a tidal wave, threatening to break me at any moment.

But just as quickly as everything began, it ended.

The room plunged into darkness as the lights in the house shuttered in the storm. Leo panted against my neck, trying to catch his breath. "The breaker is in the basement…"

With shaking legs, I extricated myself from his lap, leaning back on my heels. "I'm sorry…" I stuttered, unsure of why I felt the need to apologize, as I tried to both remember and forget what it had been like to have Leo's mouth and body pressed against mine. "I should go to bed…"

I could feel Leo sigh before I heard it escape his lips.

Was he disappointed?

Frustrated?

Embarrassed?

Angry?

In the dark, he was next to impossible to read. I hated that I felt so compelled to dissect even the smallest reaction. Why was I so desperate to understand him?

Without another word, Leo got up from the couch and made his way toward the basement stairs.

I worried I had made a mistake, initiating that kiss, lighting that fire. Could it be put out now? I had everything to lose.

I paused a moment before confirming the decision to go to his room, and leave this future in the past. Another crack of thunder made my heart pound faster.

Storm or not, I couldn't bear the thought of being rejected by Leo when he returned, so I'd deal with facing a different fear…alone.

The next morning, I felt like I had a mental hangover,

trying to wrap my brain around why I had been stupid enough to freaking kiss Leo West.

What had I been thinking?

And the worst part was that I was going to have to face him again, sooner rather than later. What was I supposed to say? That I had been drunk? I mean, I had been tipsy, but I knew exactly what I had been doing. He'd know I wasn't telling the truth if I lied and said I had been too drunk to remember.

But the worst part was the unknown. How was this going to affect us moving forward? Would he be mad? Feel taken advantage of? Embarrassed? Would he take the job from me?

Without realizing it, I'd missed our normal morning coffee as I spiraled, sitting in his bed, surrounded by him, but unable to move.

Eventually I managed to get myself dressed and peeked my head out the door. He wasn't in the kitchen. I couldn't hear him close by. So I chanced it, and quickly crossed through the living room toward the library, hoping he wasn't lying in wait for me there.

Thankfully, the library was empty when I arrived.

But it didn't stay that way for long.

"You're avoiding me," Leo accused, standing in the doorway.

The sound of his voice cutting through the quiet startled me, causing me to drop the book I'd been holding.

I spun around, expecting him to be angry. But he wasn't

mad—he looked hurt.

I said nothing, unable to feign ignorance or give some half-assed excuse.

"Or maybe you weren't in the mood for coffee?" He sighed, slowly approaching me.

I nodded, agreeing with him.

"Liar." He sulked.

I gulped. I didn't know what to do to diffuse the situation. I didn't even know what I wanted anymore.

That was another lie. I knew what I wanted. I wanted Leo. But it was too risky.

"We need to talk about last night," he said calmly, trying to gauge my reaction.

"It can't happen again," I replied instinctively, unsure of the words as they passed my lips.

"Why?" Leo's voice cracked, his brow furrowed. He continued to move toward me with slow, even steps.

"This job—it's too important to me. You're my boss— you sign my paychecks," I managed.

"I'd never take this project from you." He shook his head defensively. "Whatever happens between us—I wouldn't do that to you."

I watched him, mere steps away.

"But there *is* something between us—I know you feel it too." His tone was pleading. He needed me to validate that he wasn't alone in feeling the way he did.

I remained silent, unable to confirm or deny. I knew if

I spoke, my voice would betray me. My thundering heart might have already tipped him off if he could hear it beating out of my chest like I could.

"If I wasn't—if there wasn't…would things be different?" Leo needed to know if the job was the only thing standing between us.

Was he falling for me, like I had already fallen for him?

I felt like he couldn't let me go, but he didn't know how to move forward. I understood that he didn't want to hurt me.

I looked up at him to find he had closed the distance between us and was standing directly in front of me. My eyes pleaded with him.

Of course there was something between us, but I couldn't admit it—not out loud. If I did, there'd be no going back.

But maybe I was already too far gone. Was I in denial?

"It's different for women—you know how quickly gossip spreads in your circles. I'll get a reputation for sleeping with clients," I argued, though it was pointless. But there was a part of me that had concern over both the short- and long-term potential for my career if we took things too far and they didn't work out, or even if they did…people would talk.

"But we haven't even slept together yet," Leo argued.

"Yet…?" The word hung between us like an albatross.

Unable to hold himself back anymore, Leo leaned toward me, wrapping his arm around my waist, stopping just far enough from my lips that I had to move forward to consent…

which I did.

Pressed against the bookcase, I was helpless to deny him.

"Penny, I want you," he whispered against my skin, running his lips over the nape of my neck, then my jaw, then finally returning to my lips.

I was lost in him.

"I'll do anything," he breathed against me.

In a brief moment of sanity, I gently pushed him away.

Leo stopped immediately; he studied my face. "Pen…"

But the words died on his lips, because the moment he said my name, I couldn't help but pull him back to me. I was unable to do anything but give in to my desires.

His hands were everywhere. I needed every bit of him, and he was willing to give me whatever I wanted.

Breathless, we separated for a moment, panting against each other, our foreheads still touching.

"I'm not trying to fuck up your life, Pen, but I can't stay away from you," he professed. "I can work on getting you legal, contractual job security, so you don't have to worry about keeping the project. I'll do whatever you want. I just—I can't lose you…" I felt his lips graze my cheek.

"I need to take things slow…" I tried to find some part of my sanity to help me communicate properly.

Leo nodded against me. "Can I be close to you—when we're alone?"

"Yes," I said without hesitation.

I could feel Leo smiling against me at the speed of my

response.

"But when other people are here...you need to be careful—we both do. How we are around each other—nobody can even get a whiff of anything going on between us," I said more firmly. I didn't like the idea of having to constantly be on guard when we weren't alone, but it was a means to an end.

"I can do that..." Leo pulled back slightly, his palm cupping my cheek. "Any other terms?"

"I can't think straight…" I didn't mean to say it out loud, but the knowing smile it garnered from Leo was worth the admission.

He leaned down, kissing me gently one last time before releasing me. He sighed as he severed contact, taking a step back from me. "I should leave before I do something stupid to mess this up," he joked, running his hand through his hair nervously.

"Wait—there's something I need to talk to you about." I didn't want there to be any secrets between us. And in a matter of two days, this one had gnawed at me so profusely I couldn't keep it to myself any longer.

Leo took another step back and gestured to the seating area beside us, inviting me to sit down.

Were his legs as shaky as mine?

I felt much more composed, sitting down, and at least a foot away from Leo.

The lust and tension between us was still palpable but

dissipating as Leo seemed to read the urgency in my tone.

He leaned forward in his chair, his elbows resting on his legs. He was listening.

"I found something on Friday." I hesitated, unsure of how to tell him exactly what had happened. I realized I'd just have to start from the beginning. "I was sorting through the library and I came across a journal."

Leo raised a brow, intrigued.

"It belonged to your mom." I swallowed, waiting for the anger to come.

"Really?" He sounded surprised.

"I tried to call you," I said defensively.

"It's okay." Leo reached out, placing his palm on my forearm. "Where is it?"

I sighed. "I had it with me in my room when I fell asleep that night, but when I woke up, it was gone. I've looked everywhere, Leo. I'm so sorry." I could feel my chest tightening with anxiety.

Leo gently squeezed my arm. "Pen, it's okay. I'm not mad. But what do you think happened?"

"I don't know. When I woke up, that shadow was in my room—"

Leo's face paled. "There really was someone in your room that night…"

"I thought it was just my imagination—or a trick of the light, but it felt like something was in that corner—maybe it was a person…" I tried to run through what I remembered of that night, but it was all such a jumble of nerves I could only remember the fear I'd felt when I'd woken up and the relief when I'd found Leo downstairs.

We both took a beat.

"Do you think it was the same person who got into the solarium?" I asked.

"Maybe—I don't like the idea of someone knowing their way around this house better than me," Leo said anxiously.

Another pregnant pause enveloped the room.

"Did you read it?" Leo asked hesitantly.

I nodded slowly.

Leo sighed in relief. "Thank god—what did it say?"

He wasn't upset. I hadn't expected that. I'd spent two days convincing myself that he'd be furious with me. But he'd been understanding, open, and kind. I needed to work on giving him the benefit of the doubt more often.

I hadn't realized how much trauma I was carrying from my relationship with Adam—he always blamed me for everything. I just defaulted to protecting myself.

Leo wasn't like him—in fact he couldn't be more different.

"You okay?" Leo's hand slid down my arm to take my own.

"Yeah, just a little overwhelmed with everything," I said honestly.

Leo smiled gently.

"It started a few months before her death," I began. "It was normal at first. I wondered if maybe she was writing it for you, or to remember how you were when you were younger."

The idea perplexed Leo. So much of his mother must be an enigma to him. Everything he knew about her was through other people—their ideas of her, their perspectives. Leo hadn't been old enough to be able to make his own impressions of her.

"She loved you. She loved your father—she wished he was around more often to spend time with you, but the first half of the journal was mostly talking about your milestones, and what she was up to around the house, who she had lunch with in town, just everyday kind of stuff."

Leo sat enthralled as I told him more about his mother's state of mind, her regular routines, how she'd spent her time. I felt so guilty he couldn't read it himself.

"She often referred to someone with a symbol, instead of their name. I couldn't figure out who it was; she used gender-neutral pronouns."

"A symbol?" Leo's brow furrowed.

I got up from my chair and grabbed a notepad and pen and drew the symbol that looked like the narrow "X's" in a row, the tops and bottoms of the letters connected: ⋙.

Leo stared at the symbol. "They were skinny like that," I pointed out.

"I have no idea." He shook his head. "I've never seen it before."

"Whoever they were, they were close to Christine—she told them everything. Do you know who your mom was friends with back then? Would William know? Maybe Val?"

"Maybe…" I could see the gears turning in Leo's head, trying to think of who XXX could be, or who would know Christine's mystery friend. "Why use a code?"

"I thought the same thing. I wondered if maybe she was worried about someone finding the journal."

"So a friend she wouldn't want my father to know about?" Leo suggested.

"Or maybe the friend themselves, because halfway through writing in the journal, their relationship changed. Christine found out something X had done. Do you know anyone named Thomas and Mary?" I asked.

"My grandparents—paternal," Leo replied.

My eyes widened.

"Whoever X was, they did something to Thomas and Mary. Christine said they didn't deserve what X had done. She said if your dad found out, he'd take revenge on X, and she was terrified he'd get arrested and be taken from both you and her."

Leo remained perplexed. "Okay, so not Dad for sure then—who else was she close to?"

"Leo, nothing about this journal read as suicidal—your mom said in her last entry that she'd started to hide the journal around the house because she was scared X figured out that she knew what had happened. I think that's how it ended up in the library."

"You think she was killed." He choked.

I nodded slowly.

"Why was everyone so sure she wanted to kill herself, then?" Leo's voice trembled. Had everyone lied to him his entire life, or had none of them known Christine well enough to realize that she would never abandon him?

"Maybe they were trying to find logic to explain an illogical death," I tried, knowing that even if that was the truth, it didn't make up for everything Leo had gone through. Both of his parents had likely been murdered.

Then Leo spoke aloud what I had been silently wondering. "Do you think it was the same person…?"

"I don't know…" I shook my head. "I just know that if that journal really was Christine's, she loved you, and she never would have left you. There was nothing in that diary that made me think she would have ever considered taking her life," I said honestly.

I knew in the back of my mind, there was still a small chance that something had changed between her last entry and her last moments on Earth. Maybe I was giving him hope that would later be taken from him, but I truly believed that she hadn't left this world willingly.

"Do you think you could get access to the police report for her death? Maybe it has more information that will help you figure out what happened, now that you know more," I suggested.

"Maybe Margot or William knows someone at the station…"

"I don't know if you should involve them—we still haven't ruled them out completely," I said hesitantly.

"Right..." Leo leaned back in his chair. His world was falling apart around him, and I was the only thing helping keep him upright.

"I'm so sorry I lost the journal—if we had it, we could go to the police, maybe you'd see something I missed."

"Penny." Leo again reached for my hand. "You didn't lose the journal—someone snuck into your room while you were sleeping and took it from you. It's not your fault. None of this is your fault. I'd be lying if I said I wasn't overwhelmed with all of this new information. It's a lot—it was already a lot when I thought it was just my dad who had been murdered, but now..." He paused to take a deep breath.

"This isn't your fault either. You couldn't have stopped any of this from happening."

"Not Mom, but if I'd kept a closer watch on Dad—"

"Then whoever wanted him dead would have found another way. How could you protect him from something neither of you saw coming?"

"I know you're right." He sighed. "Val and Carl weren't much help when I asked them about what happened to Dad, but I know they both liked my mom. Maybe they'll remember something about her that can help."

"Good," I agreed.

Leo's face suddenly shot to attention. He reached into his pocket. Someone was calling him. "It's the PI," he told me before answering the call.

"Hey Greg," Leo greeted him.

A muffled response from the PI followed.

"You found her?" Leo's face lit up.

I leaned forward in anticipation.

But then Leo's face dropped. "What?" He stuttered. "When?"

I watched his expression as he grew confused, then determined. "Keep me posted. Thanks," he said curtly before ending the call.

"What happened?" I asked timidly.

"Nurse Julie was killed last night in a burglary gone wrong." Leo scowled.

I felt my heart drop. "That's awfully weird timing…"

"My thoughts exactly."

CHAPTER 9

AFTERMATH

While we waited for more information on what had happened to Julie, Leo and I fell into a sort of inelegant routine, in which he made himself scarce—I suspect because he didn't trust himself around me—while others were in the house with us. While he avoided me, I spent my days perfecting the redesigned and updated bedrooms on the second floor.

Seeing everything come together was incredibly rewarding, but the awkward fog of tension that had settled upon Willowbrooke wouldn't quite allow me to enjoy the process as much as I had hoped. Still, there were moments where I would forget everything that was going on around me and get into this zen work-mode, where creativity flowed out of me. The newly completed spaces felt like a breath of fresh air in the midst of our complicated situation.

At night, when the workers were gone, Leo would return from chasing down leads and trying to learn more about what could have happened to his parents, thirty years apart from one another. He seemed to take joy in seeing each room I completed, pointing out small details, and always needed to have a moment alone to take a deep breath and absorb the space.

After dinner, a couple glasses of wine typically led to steamy makeout sessions on the couch, most of which ended too soon for my liking, but Leo's restraint impressed me. I'd told him I wanted to take things slow, and he was waiting for permission to move past this initial phase. Unwilling to separate myself from him, I'd fall asleep next to him most nights while he read, comforted by his warmth and our growing connection.

When I was alone with my thoughts during the day, doubt would creep in, and in an effort to protect myself, I think I was almost trying to convince myself if things didn't work out between Leo and I, it was probably for the better. But when he was next to me, when he was touching me, kissing me, every single doubt melted away. Any anxiety I'd built up over the course of the day would vanish, and there was only him.

It was bliss.

Toward the end of the week, I was putting the finishing touches on the blue room, lost in thought, when Leo found me upstairs.

"This was my room growing up, you know…" Leo wrapped an arm around my waist, gently pulling my back to his front. "It's never looked better."

"Danny's downstairs," I sighed, placing my hands on his arm.

"I know," he whispered, placing soft kisses from the crook of my neck up to just below my ear. "I shut the door."

I laughed at his response. "You're home early." I turned in his arms, then pulled his face to mine for another stolen kiss.

"Greg's here," he said reluctantly, knowing the moment had now passed.

"Your PI?" I raised a brow.

Leo nodded. "He said he finally got some info from his contact at the local police. I thought you might want to join us."

"Thank you." I gave him one final peck on the lips before using the pad of my thumb to wipe my lip gloss from his mouth.

"He's in the library," Leo said. "Wait a minute, then come down."

"Okay." I smiled, willing to follow his instructions.

I fluffed some pillows and reordered a few decor pieces on the bookshelf before deciding I had waited long enough.

Down in the library, Greg Masters, Leo's PI friend,

wasn't quite what I had pictured. Perhaps I'd watched one too many noir movies, which had me anticipating a dark and brooding, broad-shouldered gentleman in a suit. Greg wasn't any of those things. Balding, with a slim build and casual attire, he stood a head below Leo, a backpack slung over one shoulder. I would have pegged him for a reporter over a private detective.

"Nice to meet you." I smiled as I shook his hand.

Greg returned the gesture, but I got the distinct impression he had been sizing me up from the moment I walked into the room. Every move I made, every word I said, was up for scrutiny. Maybe he was a PI, after all.

Leo closed the library door behind me, locking it, an action that was maybe necessary to avoid interruptions, but still seemed over-the-top.

"Can't be too careful," Greg told me, with a hard New England accent, watching my face. Leo had apparently locked the door at his behest.

"You said you have new information." Leo gestured for both of us to take a seat in the same chairs where I had confessed to finding Christine's journal after he'd kissed me against the bookshelf.

A glance in the general direction had me blushing.

Greg raised an eyebrow, unable to assign logic to my reaction.

"Initially, they thought it was a burglary gone wrong." Greg leaned back in the wingback chair. "But the nurse's husband insists that nothing was taken, there's no forced entry—in fact there was evidence that she had company."

"You mentioned she was shot?" Leo asked.

Greg nodded. "Yes, so our murderer came prepared for something."

I swallowed hard. Hearing the details like this made my stomach turn.

"You should get her some mint tea," Greg told Leo without even glancing at me.

Leo turned to me questioningly.

"It will help with the nausea," Greg answered Leo's question without having been asked.

Leo squeezed my shoulder as he got up from his seat next to me. "I'll be right back."

When Leo was out of the room, Greg asked, "How long have you two been together?"

I exhaled a shaky breath. "Not long," I replied, knowing that lying to the observant man would be pointless and might, in fact, result in him labeling me as untrustworthy. "We're trying to keep it a secret," I admitted.

Greg nodded. "Can't be too careful," he said again. "He's a good guy," he offered without prompting. "He'll be better than the dirtbag who left you."

I glared at Greg.

"I do background checks on everyone I work with." Again, the man answered my silent question. "I'd be a fool not to."

"Can't be too careful," I mimicked Greg.

He let out a boisterous cackle.

"What'd I miss?" Leo returned, taking the trouble to lock the door once again before handing me a steaming cup of tea.

"She's a good match for you," Greg told Leo.

Leo eyed me curiously as he sat down, wondering what I had divulged.

"You're not as sly as you're both trying to be," Greg pointed out.

Leo rolled his eyes. "You'll get used to him," he told me. "Can we get back to business instead of you interrogating my girlfriend?"

I almost choked on my tea, surprised by the title Leo had bestowed on me without us discussing anything of the kind first. It wasn't that I minded the label, but it was shocking nonetheless that he thought of me as such. Maybe he was just using a platitude to communicate with Greg? I'd have to tease him about it later. I looked forward to it, in fact.

"They have a suspect.".

Leo opened his mouth to ask who, but the PI was a step ahead. "You know him—William Mitchell."

"William?" Leo's face fell, and his entire body sunk into itself.

"They've got a decent amount on the guy," Greg continued. "DNA evidence from the crime scene, and supposedly they had an affair while she cared for your father, and he doesn't have a solid alibi for the murder—says he was asleep, at home, alone."

"An affair?" Leo was incredulous. "I don't—he wouldn't—they never…"

"Some people are better at hiding it than others." Greg raised a brow, clearly referring to Leo and me.

"I don't believe it," Leo said firmly, crossing his arms over his chest. "He's soft—my dad always played bad cop—the guy practically raised me—I don't think he's capable."

"I'm just presenting you the facts, Leo." Greg's tone was defensive. He was probably used to clients in denial turning on him. "DA is getting an arrest warrant as we speak. The case seems pretty straightforward."

"I never got any kind of vibe from either of them—that there would be anything—and William isn't a philanderer. He's been happily married for almost forty years."

"Kid"—Greg leaned forward—"I'm not familiar with the guy, but you know better than most that you can't know what goes on behind closed doors."

Leo sighed.

"But that's not all I found." Greg seemed nervous as he pulled a file from his backpack. "I was able to get a copy of your mother's police report." He slid the file on the coffee table in front of Leo.

"You should take a look—I removed the pictures, but if you want them, let me know," Greg said.

"No." Leo shook his head. "I don't think I could…"

"There are interview transcripts with the people that

knew her—were close to her around her death."

"Anything suspicious? Anything that stood out?" Leo rested his hand on top of the folder, too nervous to open it.

"Everyone except for your aunt was surprised about her method of death," he replied.

Leo looked up at Greg, waiting for more information.

"George wasn't around much, though he did admit that they'd drifted a bit, and that they'd been fighting about how much he worked. He said your mom wanted him to spend more time with you."

The interview corroborated what I'd learned from the journal, although Christine hadn't mentioned any fights, which did prove she was writing in a way that edited her thoughts.

"Margot said she and William were close to Christine, and that Christine had confided in her before that she had suicidal thoughts after she had given birth," Greg revealed.

"Postpartum depression is common, but it wasn't talked about as much back then," I chimed in. "Do we know if Christine ever went to therapy?"

"I'll look into it," Greg offered, seemingly disarmed that I had thought of something he hadn't considered.

"What did William say?" Leo asked.

"Not much. He said that his relationship with your mother was a surface-level friendship due to his business relationship with your father."

"So who was telling the truth? Margot or William?" I

asked.

"The truth usually lies somewhere in between," Greg offered cryptically.

Leo still seemed shell-shocked.

In the privacy of the library, knowing that Greg had already guessed our secret, I reached out to him, taking his hand in mine. He squeezed back gently, saying thank you with the gesture rather than words.

"There's one last thing," Greg said.

Leo's eyes darted across to him.

"Your dad mentioned an ex-boyfriend of your mother—Jeremy Pruitt. She had a restraining order. He began stalking her when your parents first started dating. Your father was convinced he had something to do with it, but he was in another state on business at the time, so the police dismissed him as a suspect and decided to rule her death a suicide."

"He never mentioned an ex-boyfriend or stalker—he never even told me he didn't think she had killed herself…" Leo said dejectedly.

Greg got up from his chair. "I'll look into the therapist and keep an eye on the nurse's case," he promised Leo, giving him a handshake instead of a verbal goodbye. "I'll see myself out."

"Thanks, Greg." Leo stood from his chair and watched the man as he left the library, gently closing the door in his wake. Leo locked it behind him.

Leo sunk back into the chair, his mood dour. I wasn't

sure what he'd expected the private detective to find, but that hadn't been it.

We sat in silence for a few minutes.

"What motive could Uncle William have had to kill Nurse Julie?" Leo finally shattered the library's quiet. "Let's say they did have an affair—why kill her now?"

"Because we started asking about her…" I was hesitant to say it out loud, but we both knew it to be true.

"Okay—let's follow that thread," Leo tried. I could see him kicking into his own sort of detective mode, the same way he had the night we'd discussed his father's death—he was disassociating. "What could she know—or say—today that she wouldn't have said before?"

"If they were in it together—the nurse didn't have a motive to kill George, but if they were having an affair, maybe he convinced her to do it." It felt silly to suggest.

Maybe I was in denial with Leo or just wanted him to be right, but I wasn't sure I believed William was responsible for any of it—the truth, however, was that I didn't know him.

Leo certainly knew him better, but all parents keep secrets from their children. William had been a father figure to Leo, so of course he would have kept the sordid details of his personal life from his adopted son.

"So what does Julie get out of it? She was still with her husband when she died." Leo was getting upset, but I knew his anger wasn't directed at me.

"Maybe money?" I tried. "I'm on your side, Leo. I don't

think William did this, but if the cops have evidence he was at her house—"

"What if he went there because he knew I was looking for her? Maybe he was trying to get her to talk to us."

"Maybe." I shrugged.

Leo's shoulders slumped as he hunched in the chair, completely out of sorts. "And I don't know what to make of my mom's file. I didn't know that Margot and my mom were so close—and I've never heard of this Jeremy Pruitt guy—but I'm not surprised that Dad never mentioned anything. We never talked about Mom's death."

"I'm sorry," I said softly, placing a hand on his knee.

Leo moved to take my hand in his when a knock at the library door shocked the two of us apart.

Concerned, Leo bolted to the door and opened it to find his Aunt Margot.

"Why on earth did you lock the door?" She laughed, then saw me, and her face dropped for a moment before a grin replaced her surprise. "Hello, dear." She beamed. "I saw your work upstairs—fabulous job."

"Thank you, Margot." I smiled politely.

"To what do I owe the pleasure?" Leo gave his aunt a hug. While in her embrace, his eyes met mine, then nervously darted down to the file folder on the coffee table.

I swiftly grabbed the papers and sat on them.

"I was worried I've been absent too long with all the planning for the gala—I've barely seen you in the last few weeks, so I thought I'd stop by." Margot set to correcting Leo's lapels, which had been rumpled during their hug.

"It's alright," Leo told her. "Is everything going okay?"

"Oh you know—planning these things should be straightforward, but they never are." Margot turned to address me.

I hoped my face wasn't beet red, knowing I was intentionally hiding something from her in plain sight.

"Will you be joining us on Saturday evening?" Margot asked.

"I—uhh." I looked past Margot to Leo. "I didn't know I was invited."

Margot's laugh tinkled through the room. "Of course, darling, any friend of Leo's is invited, and I've got a few more people who are interested in hiring you—it will be a good time to meet them. Get this business of yours started."

Leo raised a brow at her last comment. "We'll see, Aunt Margot," he stepped in, saving me.

"I need to know by the end of day tomorrow to finalize the seating chart," she told him pointedly.

"I promise."

"Now that I'll have an extra seat, what with William no longer attending—"

"Why?" Leo asked.

"You haven't heard?" Margot's eyes bulged. She was in her element spreading gossip. I had thought that she and William were friendly, but his change in fortune allowed for a break in standard protocol.

Leo shook his head. Of course he had an inkling of what was going on, but he didn't want to explain how or why to Margot.

"Sweetheart"—she cupped his cheek with her palm—"he was arrested this afternoon. They think he murdered your father's nurse."

"Is he going to be okay?" Leo's reaction was genuine.

"He'll probably be able to get out on bail. They won't make him stay in jail, if that's what you mean," Margot replied solemnly.

Leo stepped back. "I heard she died, but I thought it was a botched robbery."

"They'd been having an affair," Margot revealed. "I knew about it while she was here, but it wasn't my place—poor Alicia." Margot turned to me. "Alicia is William's wife."

I nodded in understanding.

"William's always been a bit of a playboy—going after women that were married for sport. Of course George never liked it, but there was too much history—too much money at stake. So he let it slide." She sighed.

"I think Alicia's always known—perhaps they have an agreement, one of those things they just didn't discuss as long as he paid the bills and didn't let things go public. He used to be more discreet, but maybe he's losing his touch in his old age."

"William always seemed so devoted to his wife," Leo

disagreed.

"Appearances, Leo—they're so important in our circles. You saw exactly what they wanted you to see."

Margot paused suddenly, spotting something on the desk. She stepped over to examine it. "I haven't seen this in a while." She pointed.

I stayed put, not wanting to expose the file folder beneath me.

Leo joined her at the desk. "Oh, I saw it in one of the books while we were cataloging them."

Leo raised the notepad, where I had written the XXX symbol I'd found in Christine's journal. My eyes widened involuntarily.

"You know what it is?" Leo said, trying to keep the earnestness from his voice, but failing miserably.

"Oh sure—they're William's initials—he talked about using it as the logo for his company when we were growing up, but then when he and George went into business together, they had to pick a name that represented both of them," Margot replied matter-of-factly.

"It's a W and an M overlapping." She took the pen from the desk, and I watched from afar as she showed Leo how they were written to form what I had previously thought were the consecutive "X's."

"Huh…" Leo stared down at the paper.

"Shame on him for writing in one of these books though—must have done it when we were children," Margot scolded.

"Anyway, I'd better get going." Margot began the trek across the room. "Leo, let me know when you are free for lunch next week—I'd love to catch up."

"Of course," he acquiesced.

"And do let me know if you'll be joining us at the gala." Margot turned her attention to me.

I nodded in agreement.

"I'll walk you out." Leo held the door open for his aunt.

"Thank you, dear." She smiled up at him. "Good afternoon, Penny."

I gave her a small wave, before releasing a long exhale the moment she was out of earshot.

Leo returned a few moments later, still out of sorts.

"Can you hide the folder in my room?" he asked, looking down at the papers I clutched to my chest. I couldn't lose it like I had lost the journal.

"Sure."

"And we're going to talk about this business of yours when I get back," he threatened.

"There is no business—I keep telling her that. I don't know a thing about how to run a company. I'm just a designer." My brow furrowed as he turned on his heel to leave. "Wait—where are you going?"

"I need to go down to the station and see if I can bail out William—I have to talk to him," Leo said hurriedly.

"I can go with you—"

"No," he said bluntly, then took a deep breath and adjusted his tone. "Please stay here. I'll keep you updated. My phone is fully charged," he promised.

"Be safe," I said, but he was already down the hall.

Waiting for Leo to return was a bit nerve-wracking. It felt like things were going off the rails, and we were helpless to stop them. I knew Leo probably felt even more out of control than I did.

Danny was hesitant to leave for the day, sensing something wasn't right, but I assured him I would be okay and again found myself alone in the house as the sun set. Tendrils of darkness encroached upon the main floor, which I fought against by turning on as many lights as I could find.

Not wanting to bother Leo, I resolved not to text him asking for an update, knowing if he had one, he would contact me. As the minutes ticked by, and he still hadn't returned, I decided to keep myself distracted by attempting to make dinner. I wasn't a terrible cook, but I certainly wasn't as skilled or remotely as passionate as Leo was when it came to the kitchen.

I opted for a simple dinner of roasted carrots and braised chicken. Leo had shown me how to make it only a week before. My attempt wasn't as good as his, but it was passable.

With impeccable timing, Leo arrived just as I was pulling the carrots from the oven.

"You made dinner…" His tone was grateful, but his appearance betrayed him, showing his exhaustion as he approached me in the kitchen.

"It's not as good as—"

Before I could say "yours," Leo wrapped me up in a tight hug.

"You made dinner…" he whispered into my hair, refusing to let me go.

But I didn't mind, and I gladly returned the embrace.

"Are you okay?" I pulled back slightly, brushing some stray hair from his eyes. "Is William okay?"

Leo nodded, finally releasing me from his hold.

"His lawyer wouldn't let me talk to him, but they're processing his release on bail." Leo slumped into one of the barstools.

"That's good, right?" I pulled the chicken from the burner before removing a wineglass from the dishwasher and giving Leo a generous pour of red wine.

"It's something…" He sighed after taking a long pull from the glass.

"We don't have to talk about it, if you don't want to." He wasn't obligated to keep me informed of every small detail, especially since he was swimming in so much uncertainty; the stress was written all over his face.

"You sure?" he asked, grateful for the reprieve.

I smiled, nodding. "I'm here, whatever you want to talk about—or not talk about."

Taking me up on my invitation, dinner was a quiet affair, but Leo made sure I knew how thankful he was for my efforts, despite my perceived shortcomings. I would have thought it was the best meal he'd ever had, if I hadn't eaten every dish he'd served me before.

But after dinner, when we'd usually retire to the couch to continue talking over a glass of wine, Leo caught me off guard when he asked if we could instead lie down in the room.

"I'm just tired…" he breathed, his voice unable to hide the depth of truth in his statement.

That first night, lying together in his bed, a moment which I had been thinking of since the first night I'd spent alone there, didn't play out the way I had expected, but perhaps just snuggling and falling asleep was exactly what I needed.

Despite his insomnia, Leo easily fell asleep in my arms.

CHAPTER 10

LAID BARE

I was surprised to find Leo gone by the time I woke up the next morning. There was a note next to a fresh pot of coffee with his apologies. He had an appointment he'd forgotten about and would return later—his phone was fully charged.

Doing a final walk-through of the second floor with Danny took up most of my day. Leo sent a text in the afternoon letting me know he'd take care of dinner and that he missed me. The latter part sent my heart soaring.

Despite my best efforts to quell my feelings, I had fallen for Leo so quickly, and so hard, I was worried about the damage it would cause if things didn't work out. I didn't think I'd ever get over Leo if he rejected me.

As promised, Leo returned in the evening with takeout, but was mum on where he'd been all day.

"Did you get a chance to talk to William?" I asked, wondering why he wasn't sharing his whereabouts, when he was normally an open book with me.

Leo shook his head. "I'll tell you after dinner—I want to hear about your day," he changed the subject.

Annoyed, but knowing he'd be good on his word, I ran through the short list of fixes Danny and I had located upstairs, wanting to wrap everything up before flooring work began on the first level in another week.

After we finished eating, Leo took our dishes to the kitchen and returned with refilled glasses of wine and a manilla envelope tucked under one arm.

I followed him closely as he handed me my glass, then removed the envelope from his hold. He slid a pen across the coffee table along with it.

"What's in there?" I asked.

Leo leaned back into the couch and took a drink of wine before replying, "It's an updated contract for you."

He tried to hide a smile, but I had pierced the veil of many of his tells since we'd admitted our feelings for one another.

I set my glass down and took the envelope, slowly opening it and pulling the paperclipped pages from it. "What does it say?" I flipped through the papers, but wanted to hear it from him.

"You'll be contractually hired by the trust to conduct the renovations and redesign. As an employee of the trust, multiple people will have to sign off on any changes to your employment status," he answered.

"Which means...?"

"I alone have no power to remove you from the project, if you sign that document. The trust will be your client, not me. Your pay will come directly from the trust, not me. I will no longer be your direct boss or hold any controlling influence over your tenure working on the house." His grin was wide as he took another sip of his wine.

Once I signed that document, there would be nothing between us. Nothing to stop me from pursuing him. No fears of repercussions on the project. There would always be the threat of gossip in the circles his family ran in, but I knew he'd protect me as well as he could. And even if things went south, I'd always have Willowbrooke on my resume, a fair start to my career with or without his help or influence.

I should have reviewed the document, asked Mina if her lawyer boyfriend could make sure I was protected enough, but I didn't care—I trusted Leo had my best interest at heart. Without looking at it, I signed on the dotted line and pushed the papers back across the coffee table toward Leo.

"What if I still want you to be the boss?" I teased playfully.

"That can be arranged," Leo replied coyly, taking a final pull of his wine and setting the empty glass on the coffee table, before slowly leaning forward and taking my half-full glass from me, his fingers grazing mine. He placed it next to his.

I watched, frozen, as Leo slowly moved toward me. Then without warning, he was on me. One hand weaved through my hair, pulling me to him, as he teased my mouth open with his. The other snaked around my waist, holding me close as he pushed me back into the couch, settling between my legs, which I instinctively wrapped around his hips, silently pleading for him to come closer.

His searing, maddening kiss was undoing me. Heat pooled low, a coil wound tightly, every nerve ending in my body responding eagerly to his touch. Before, exchanges like this had always had an expiration date—a boundary that couldn't be crossed, but it was gone now.

I made quick work of unbuttoning his shirt. Only one more layer stood between me and his skin. I was lost to his ministrations as his mouth found purchase at every nook and cranny available to him.

A low and heady moan stifled the air, and Leo chuckled against me as I realized the sound had come from me. Unaware of the passage of time, Leo and I could have been kissing for seconds, minutes, or hours, but when he drew back, I protested.

Leo only smiled conspiratorially as he ran his hands along my bare thighs. I had changed into a pajama shirt and shorts before dinner. He gently tugged my legs from around his hips, which garnered another moan of disapproval from me.

"Leo…" I pleaded—for what, I'm still not certain.

His hands on the crook of my knees, Leo repositioned himself lower. My breath hitched when his fingers slid up to my hips, hooking themselves onto the edge of my shorts and panties at the same time. He glanced up at me briefly, giving me the opportunity to stop him, but I was too enraptured in what would come next to do anything but try to slow my panting.

Dragging the fabric down my legs, over my knees, and then off me completely, he discarded them on the floor. Leo pulled me toward him so my back was lying flat on the couch, before hooking my knees over his shoulders, as he lay on his stomach. A moment later, I felt his warm breath caressing me, just before his mouth found my core.

I bucked at the sensation, and Leo stilled, clamping one hand tightly around my leg, while using the other to accompany the attention of his tongue against me. I was immediately lost in the dance, unable to focus on anything but my building climax.

Daring to watch, I let my eyes slide toward him, and I found his darkened gaze locked on mine, challenging me, proud of his victory, claiming what he wanted without abandon.

"Fuck…" I hissed, as one of his fingers easily slid into me, shortly matched by a second, dragging against me from the inside, while Leo's mouth slowly moved closer to the spot he knew would finish us both. And when he made it there, it only took a split second for the coil to snap. My body trembled beneath him, and he continued his movements, wanting to extend my pleasure as far as it would stretch.

Leo slowed at the same pace as my breathing, finally withdrawing from me, and his cocky grin, now seemingly permanently affixed to his face, had me briefly questioning why he had just done what he had…and why I'd let him.

Before any doubt or embarrassment could seep in, Leo wiped his arm across his mouth, leaning down to kiss me again, gently…slowly…a preview of the pace to come. "Let me clean you up," he whispered. "I've made a mess of you."

But when he tried to pull away, I stopped him. "Can we go to the room?" I asked softly.

I wasn't finished with him yet.

He nodded, offering me a hand as he extricated himself from on top of me. I was appreciative of the gesture, as my legs were unsteady as a result of his activities.

Once in the room, I kneeled at the end of the bed, drawing him against me, as he still stood.

I pulled his undershirt over his head. Feeling the heat from his chest made me want to burrow inside him and never leave.

I'd soon get my chance.

I felt him tug at the hem of my oversized night shirt—a soft old concert tee. "It's only fair," he whispered against my ear.

I lifted my arms, allowing him to remove it from me. We really were skin to skin then, but he was still wearing pants. I wasn't close enough.

While he used his mouth to explore my breasts, I worked to unfasten his belt, then his zipper. He stepped out of his pants, gently helping me recline on the bed, with him still on top of me.

"Condom?" I murmured against him, my legs again finding purchase around his hips, keeping him as close as possible.

Without leaving his position above me, he reached out to the nightstand, feeling around the top drawer until he was able to pull one out from the back and hand it to me.

We worked together to free him from his boxer briefs and utilize the condom. He needed no help preparing himself for me otherwise.

Feeling him slide inside me was heaven. He was so close, peppering me with gentle, languid kisses and caresses, whispering adoring words as he moved within me.

I thought I'd known Leo West before that moment, but I'd had no idea.

I hadn't expected making love with him to be so sweet, so slow, so emotional, so very intimate.

It was like nothing I had experienced before.

And as we came together in one final climax, I couldn't help but feel like it was so much more than my body he had penetrated that night; he had reached something deep inside me, a place where nobody had been before, a place I had never allowed anyone to enter. I had let him in willingly, and I knew I'd fight to let him stay there. I had given him a piece of myself that had never and would never belong to anyone else.

Drifting off, naked and spent, in Leo's arms, I felt satiated for the first time, finally knowing what it felt to love someone who loved me in return. I could have sworn as I faded from consciousness that I heard him say he felt it too...

The next morning, I couldn't help myself from initiating a sleepy and slow second round. Leo's breathy moans, while I used my mouth to conduct some exploring of my own, were well worth the effort, before he helped me straddle him, holding my hands and watching me closely as I rocked against him, bringing us both to another euphoric release.

He was everything. I couldn't get enough of him.

Unfortunately our post-coital, pre-coffee cuddling was cut short when he received a text from William, who was on his way over, against the advice of counsel.

"I'll make it up to you," Leo apologized as we helped each other dress.

"It's okay," I assured him.

Leo made quick work of tidying the mess we'd left behind in the kitchen and living room the night before. Luckily, I spotted my missing panties and shorts tucked under one of the curtains mere moments before William arrived.

William was unusually discombobulated when he appeared. While he still looked tidy in his business suit and tie, his face was drawn, with deep circles under his eyes and his mouth set in an unnaturally thin line.

I made myself busy pouring a round of coffee for everyone. I thought William might ask me to leave, or feel awkward because of my presence, but he greeted me warmly and was appreciative of the coffee, and took me up on my offer of some breakfast pastries, which Val had conveniently purchased the day before, while at the farmer's market.

"I'm glad you came," Leo told William. "I know your lawyer won't be pleased."

"He means well, but he doesn't know you. I'm not concerned by what you know—and I want you to know everything." William made his intent very clear. "Can you tell me what you've heard thus far?"

Leo glanced at me before relaying what we'd learned, both from the PI as well as Margot's town gossip. As he proceeded, William's shoulders slouched. It was worse than he'd feared. He hadn't anticipated that the news would move so quickly, but didn't seem surprised that Margot had been the messenger.

"None of it's true—that's the first thing you need to know," William stated. "You can choose to believe me or not, but I love my wife and have never stepped out on her. I haven't seen Julie Sullivan since your father's funeral, and I certainly have never physically harmed a single person in my entire life." He was resolute, but sounded exasperated.

"How do you think the evidence was found at her home?" Leo asked.

William shrugged. "I can only assume I'm being set up."

"Why would someone want to do this to you—who would do this to you?"

William closed his eyes and took a deep breath. "I don't know—I'm sure I've crossed people over business, but none that I would suspect would try to so thoroughly ruin my life like this." He began to pick apart his croissant, leaving flakes scattered across the plate as he went.

"How can I help you? How can I make this right?" Leo clearly felt responsible for what was happening to William. But it wasn't his fault, it was the person or persons behind everything—they had made the decision to hurt people, not Leo.

"You've done what you can, son." William clapped a palm over Leo's shoulder. "You didn't have to come the other night, but you did. I won't soon forget your loyalty."

"I'm afraid I have more questions, but they're not exactly about what happened to Julie," Leo said slowly. I knew Leo was wary about bringing up what he and I had been investigating, but if he didn't ask now, we might not get another chance.

"You want to know about Christine…" William sighed, knowing it was bound to come up sooner than later.

"We've been poking around after learning some things…" Leo was cryptic.

"What things exactly?"

Leo glanced at me, silently asking permission to mention the diary. I nodded subtly.

"Penny found my mom's journal, and it had entries from the months before her death," Leo revealed.

William raised a brow, genuinely surprised. "What did it say?"

"She wasn't suicidal," I replied.

William turned his attention to me.

"No, I don't suppose she was," William agreed.

"Why did you and Dad let me believe that my whole life, then?" Leo's tone betrayed his anger.

"Because the alternative would have been worse—to tell you that George suspected she had been murdered and that the police had done nothing. How would that have made anything better?"

"At least it would have been the truth," Leo growled scornfully.

William took another sip of his coffee. "Neither of us wanted to lie to you—in truth, I think George hoped he'd solve it on his own and then be able to tell you everything, but the longer it took—the colder the case grew…he just decided it would be better to let you believe the official story."

"Do you recognize this symbol?" Leo grabbed a memo pad and pen from the entryway table and drew the overlapping

W and M.

"No." William shook his head. "Should I?"

Leo looked at me, brow furrowed. "Aunt Margot said you used to draw it, that it was your initials."

William looked at it again. "Maybe when I was a child—I grew up with George and Margot—honestly, I don't remember it." He seemed bewildered by the monogram, but he hadn't adamantly denied it was his.

"Tell me more about Dad's investigation," Leo demanded, though I didn't think he'd meant to.

"I'll do you one better, I'll show you." William rose from the barstool. "Follow me." He motioned, when Leo and I merely stared at him without moving.

Leo grabbed my hand as he passed me, squeezing it gently to reassure me as we trailed behind William.

When I hesitated as William opened the door to the basement, Leo turned back. "You don't have to." He knew I hated it down there.

"No, I'll go." I swallowed hard.

I reminded myself that nothing was down there and that both Leo and William would be there with me.

Still, the musty, damp, heavy weight of the lower level immediately enveloped me only a few steps down the staircase. I released Leo to use the railings to steady myself, but he quickly found my hand again when we were at the bottom. Maybe he was drawing as much comfort from me as I was in him.

William turned on the available lights as he went, but the space remained murky and dank, almost as if in rebellion. He approached a bookcase, and managed to easily push it to the side, as the baseboard of the shelf was concealing casters. Moving it revealed a room previously hidden from view.

"You've got to be kidding me," Leo breathed in shock.

"A lot of old houses like this were retrofitted with hidden storage and tunnels during prohibition." William stood aside, allowing Leo and I to enter the room after he'd flipped on another too-dim lightbulb overhead.

The room had no windows and couldn't have been larger than ten square feet. The walls were plastered with notes, newspaper clippings, photographs, and other ramblings of a madman. A long folding table in the middle of the space was stacked with binders, folders, and papers in some kind of organized chaos. Behind the desk was the lone missing dining chair I'd been trying to find for weeks. I never would have found it otherwise.

"What is this place?" I let my eyes wander the packed space, not knowing where to look next.

"George only told me when he was too weak to come down here by himself," William admitted. "He called it his investigation den—decades of work trying to figure out what happened to your mother." He turned to Leo. "He never did find anything concrete enough to go to the police, but he had his theories."

Leo had approached one of the walls, where most of the

photos were taped. "I can see that." He examined the images. "You're on his list of suspects." Leo pointed to an old photo of William. There were sticky notes next to the photo that said "Motive?" and "Confirmed in-person meeting with investors at T.O.D."

"What's T.O.D.?" I asked.

"Time of death," William answered. "George told me he had long ruled me out, but he didn't want to trust anyone with what he was doing until he had something more solid… only that day never came."

"Margot's on here too," Leo commented.

The note next to her photo said, "How close were they?" and "Confirmed out of country with Ted."

"Even you're on there." William pointed to a small picture of Leo as a toddler in a corner, almost hidden by other notes.

The note next to Leo read "Confirmed with nanny at park, on playdate.'"

"He exhausted every avenue—left no stone unturned," William said.

"It looks like these two were his main targets." Leo shuffled to view the center of the wall, where larger photos of two men were positioned. Under each was a name: Jeremy Pruitt and Warren Kane. I recognized the former from the police file Leo's PI had unearthed.

"Warren Kane—is that Kane Industries?" Leo turned to William.

William nodded. "He was our primary business rival

at the time—he died in a plane crash about ten years after Christine died. I didn't like the guy, he was a prick, but I never got the impression he'd cross that kind of line—still, he took a lot of secrets to his grave, and George could never manage to get a solid alibi from him.

"Every time they spoke, it was something else. He had a different meeting on his work calendar from his personal calendar, and his personal assistant said he was with his mistress at the time, but George never found her, and Kane—he was an asshole. I think he was amused by your father's obsession with him, but murder—he was the type to initiate a hostile takeover, not kill his adversary's wife. He'd want a business victory, not a personal one."

William's phone began to ring, echoing menacingly in the enclosed space. He looked at the caller ID and declined the call. "It's my lawyer—I can't stay." He frowned.

"William…" Leo faltered. "There's something else…" He looked down at his feet, then up at me, needing a boost of confidence, which I provided with a reassuring smile.

"I think someone killed Dad."

William took a step back, alarmed by the declaration. "But the cancer—"

"The cancer was real, but he'd secretly asked me to conduct a private autopsy, and multiple pathologists think he was likely smothered." Leo raked his hand through his hair nervously.

William was silent for a minute, trying to take in

everything.

"I wondered when I first heard, but they declared it a natural death so quickly, I was almost relieved. I saw him that day; he seemed in good spirits, that's why it caught me off guard when Margot called me to tell me." William's face clouded as he recalled that day.

"You were the last person to see him alive—the nurse found him an hour later, and he was gone."

"The dead nurse…"

"You know I have to ask," Leo said painfully.

"I know." William's eyes met Leo's. "Your father was alive and as well as he could be, given his diagnosis, when I left him."

"And the nurse—I know you didn't have an affair with her, but what was your impression of her?" Leo asked.

William took a beat to think about the question. "She joked with him, but was professional. I had confidence she knew what she was doing, and I was glad she was willing to put up with his shit." William released a humorless laugh, recalling his best friend and business partner. "But I suppose, people like her, they fade into the background so easily. I never paid much attention to her. Never got to know her beyond George's treatment plan and schedule."

Leo nodded. He'd had the same experience with the woman.

William looked down at his phone again; it had chirped with a voicemail alert.

"I need to get going," William said regretfully.

"If you need anything—" Leo offered.

"I will." William gave him an understanding smile. Then he turned to me. "Take care of him, young lady."

I grinned.

"You lucked out with her." He turned back to Leo. "Don't let her get away."

Leo sighed through a smile, giving William a small wave as he backed out of the room, his footsteps dissipating as he ascended the stairs, leaving the two of us alone again.

"You heard him," I joked. "You are *so* lucky."

Leo closed the space between us, sweeping me into a hug, holding me tightly. He was upset and needed physical comfort. I returned the embrace.

"Very lucky…" he whispered, placing a soft kiss just below my ear, before stepping back. "I knew my dad was secretive, but I didn't expect him to have a hidden lair."

"Hope you didn't have any plans for the day," I laughed, picking up a folder from the desk.

"You're willing to stay down here?" he asked seriously.

"We wanted answers, and we suddenly have the opportunity to get inside the mind of a dead man." I cringed at the last two words—I hadn't been thinking.

Leo didn't seem to notice and took no offense. "There's a lot to go through. What are we looking for exactly?" He began to examine the document piles on the desk.

"I'm not sure…" I trailed off. "But I do think William is

right, your dad wouldn't have told him about this place if he suspected him of hurting your mom."

"True—but that doesn't mean he couldn't have been responsible for what happened to Dad. We assumed it was the same person who committed both crimes, but it could have been different offenders." Leo sighed.

Even with all the new information we had in front of us, I still felt like we were back at square one. I was overwhelmed with the possibilities, and the danger that still loomed over us.

For quite a few hours, Leo and I busied ourselves trying to make some sort of sense of how George had organized everything in his secret room. We shared insights as we discovered them, but came across nothing definitive that altered our perception of either death.

Mid-afternoon, the doorbell rang. Leo went to answer it, but I insisted on getting it, as I was unwilling to stay in the basement alone, even for a moment.

"Alright," he conceded. "Any chance you'd bring down something for lunch? I'm starving."

As if on cue, his stomach growled, leaving us both laughing.

On my way upstairs, I noticed something odd across the basement, along the far wall from George's hideout. There was a mark scraped along the floor, as if someone had moved something recently, but I didn't recall Leo or any of the workmen being down there. The wall was empty, with no furniture that could easily explain the size and shape of the mark in the floor. The thought nagged at me as I made my way to the front door.

A delivery driver had an overnight package addressed to Leo that requested signature service. I didn't think he was expecting anything, and I usually put my name on all orders for the house. I thought maybe it was an early Christmas present and set it aside to make a quick and late lunch for myself and Leo.

I had just finished gathering everything when I realized why the spot in the basement stood out. I recalled going through different versions of the blueprints I had ordered when I first started working at Willowbrooke, and noticed an anomaly in the basement between the original floor plans and one from the 1950's.

Precariously balancing two plates and two bottles of water, I stopped by the library, where I had stored the printouts on my way back to Leo, intent on re-examining them with him.

"Who was it?" he asked, helping relieve me of the plates.

"A delivery—required a signature." I raised a brow at him, wondering if he'd share what he'd ordered.

Leo shrugged. "Probably some wine someone sent over—that always needs a signature upon delivery." He motioned to the poster tube under my arm. "What's that?"

"There's something weird on the other side of the basement. I thought I saw something on the blueprints for the house that might explain it."

Over sandwiches, we tried to locate the discrepancies between the various versions, and finally, I found what I'd been looking for. "See, there's this indent that wasn't there in the original plans." I pointed to the almost insignificant change.

"Show me." Leo stood from his chair, gesturing for me to proceed.

I made my way across the basement and found the scrape marks I'd seen while I was going upstairs. "I haven't moved anything over here, have you?" I pointed to the marks, which were in a curved pattern, as if we stood in front of a door that had opened toward us. But in front of us was a brick wall.

"It wasn't me—and none of the guys would have any reason to come down here." Leo took out his phone and turned on the flashlight, using the light to examine the wall.

After a moment, he exclaimed, "There's a seam!"

Sure enough, with the light shining directly onto a specific line of grout, from a precise angle, you could see a slight shadow.

"How do we open it?" I began looking around for anything that stood out, pressing against the brick wall, until I realized the wall seemed to have a bit more give when I pressed near the seam. When I pushed hard enough, there was a click, like a cabinet with a magnetic latch, and the seam expanded just enough to fit my fingers into, to pry the entrance open.

"What the fuck?" Leo shone his flashlight into the abyss.

We couldn't see where the space ended.

"William said there could be prohibition tunnels." I could feel my heart beating in my chest. The darkness felt sinister, and I wanted to get as far from it as I could.

"Now we know how someone was getting in here," Leo spat bitterly.

Suddenly his phone alarm rang out, startling him enough that he dropped his phone. "Shit," he swore as he bent down to pick it up. Luckily, it hadn't sustained any damage, thanks to his case.

"What's the alarm for?" I asked, stepping back from the dark entrance.

Leo looked up at me impishly. "The gala."

"The gala," I repeated.

Leo took a look down the tunnel before latching the door in place. "We'll have to come back—we need to get ready. Margot will kill me if we're late."

"We?" I asked. I'd forgotten about Margot's invitation, assuming it had merely been a courtesy and that Leo would send her my regrets, much to her relief.

"If you think I'm going to suffer alone with a bunch of blue-hairs and social climbers, you're mistaken." He took my hand and led us back toward the staircase.

"It's black tie." I frowned. I didn't think they'd let me through the door in jeans and a blazer, which was currently the fanciest clothing I owned.

"I know." He closed the basement door behind me, attempting to hide a mischievous smile.

CHAPTER 11

THE GALA

"Where'd you put the delivery?" Leo asked, setting our empty plates in the sink.

"What did you do?" I handed him the box nervously.

He set the box on the kitchen counter before retrieving a box cutter from the entryway table. "Listen, I had help—I won't take all the blame for this." Leo opened the package and pulled out a white box with a black ribbon, which he handed to me. "I was given options and chose the one I liked best."

I looked down at the box, afraid to open it. "Help from whom?" I looked back up at Leo.

"Mina," he replied with a Cheshire smile.

My mouth gaped. "How? When?" I stammered. I was even more shocked that she had managed to keep it all a secret from me. She was terrible at keeping things from me.

"I stole your phone while you were sleeping last week," he answered sheepishly.

If I hadn't been so stunned, I would have been impressed. "I have a pin," I argued.

"And you don't pay attention when someone watches you enter it." He leaned against the counter, proud of himself. "Aren't you going to open it?"

I looked down at the box again, afraid of what I might find inside. "Schrodinger's outfit," I joked, fiddling with the black ribbon.

"Schrodinger's dress," Leo corrected me.

I sighed. A dress…I wasn't exactly a dress kind of girl, but he'd gone to so much trouble…

I pulled at the ribbon, undoing the bow, and lifted the top from the box, squinting, afraid to see the contents.

Immediately I could see Mina's handiwork. She had included the proper undergarments and accessories, a thoughtful touch. But the pièce de résistance was a royal blue dress with a low V-neck in the front, as well as a side slit, and a dangerously deep keyhole cutout in the back. She knew me well. The dress was timeless, chic, and simple.

Leo waited with bated breath for my response. "I thought the blue would bring out your eyes," he commented quietly, gently tucking a strand of hair behind my ear.

"It's beautiful," I exhaled. Peeking inside the shoe box tucked in the bottom corner, I saw Mina had chosen nude patent leather heels of a modest height, just high enough that she knew I could manage for an evening if I wasn't standing the whole time.

"Are you mad?" Leo bit his cheek, preparing himself for my wrath.

"I guess you'll find out, won't you?" I teased.

But he knew I wasn't angry. He tugged at the waist of my jeans, pulling me to him. "Promise?" He challenged, nipping at me.

"How long do we have to stay?" I simpered.

"There'll be dinner and Margot will give some sort of speech about Dad and the charity. After that, we can slip out when she's finished," he whispered, placing soft kisses along the crook of my neck.

"Think you can wait that long?" I raised a brow. "You know we'll have to keep our distance."

Leo sighed. "I know, but I might have to steal you for a dance or two."

"We'll see." I stepped back and picked up the box. "How long do I have to get ready?"

"The town car will be here in about two hours."

"Oh good, we've got time for you to join me in the shower, then," I purred.

Leo grabbed the box from me with one hand, and my wrist with the other, leading me into his bedroom for round three…which was a real doozy.

"I'm counting down the minutes until I get to help you out of that dress," Leo whispered, leaning forward as he assisted me from the town car outside the hotel.

"Well, we have to make it through the night first," I challenged. But I would have been lying if I wasn't thinking the same thing about Leo and his tuxedo. I'd never seen him look so dashing.

"Don't stare," I hissed as we made our way through the lobby. "Remember the rules."

"I remember," Leo chuckled, putting another foot between us.

I was nervous heading into the grand ballroom of the town's famous historic hotel. Not just because I wasn't sure how subtle the two of us could be around each other, but because I was acutely aware of the type of event it was, and the type of people who would be there.

If Queen Bee Margot was any indication, I would be immediately scrutinized and discussed by every single person in the room, as an outsider, a stranger, and for all intents and purposes, working class, compared to their extravagant, leisurely lives.

Although I wasn't arriving directly on Leo's arm, I was his guest, another fact that would be dissected. As the heir to the West family fortune and the archetypal prodigal son, I was sure there would be no shortage of interest at his return to society after more than a decade.

The palatial grand ballroom lived up to its name, with multiple opulent crystalline chandeliers dotting the ceiling, parquet flooring, and vintage furniture adorning the spaces not taken up with dining tables or food stations. At the stage situated at the far end of the room, a chamber orchestra played under the din of voices, air kisses, and networking.

Immediately upon entering, Leo and I were offered champagne from one of the dozen or so servers circulating with trays full of glasses. I was all too pleased to take a glass for myself, needing some liquid courage to proceed.

"I can make some introductions if you'd like," Leo offered.

I didn't want to leave his side; I felt overwhelmed and anxious at the thought of being on my own, but the closer we stuck together, the more people would talk…the more likely rumors were to develop and spread.

"Goodness, the two of you clean up nicely." Margot found us before I could reply to Leo. "Darling, you look radiant in blue—what a spectacular choice."

I blushed, not because of the compliment, but because it was Leo that had chosen both the color and the gown on my behalf, thanks to Mina's excellent taste and knowledge of my lack of fashion expertise.

"Thank you, Margot." I smiled.

"I'm stealing your date," Margot informed Leo.

Leo opened his mouth to answer his aunt, but the words

died on his lips as she whisked me away before he could get out a single syllable.

For the next hour or so, I shook hands with countless people, and was pleasantly surprised by Margot's flattering description of the work I had done at Willowbrooke. I hadn't expected her to become somewhat of a champion for my skills, but I was thankful for the opportunity and access to her immense network.

Leo and I were seated next to each other at dinner, which became more challenging than necessary when he'd occasionally and very much intentionally brush against me under the table. He knew I couldn't admonish him in front of others. I think he enjoyed the fact that I was helpless to stop him. I resolved to find a way to retaliate later.

After dinner, people resumed mingling, some couples made it to the dance floor, and I excused myself to the bathroom to take a moment for myself, feeling more than buzzed from the amount of champagne I had inadvertently consumed. The waiters had just kept replacing my glass, and I'd lost count of how many I'd imbibed.

Returning to the ballroom, I spotted Leo at the bar being chatted up by none other than Margot's surprise guest from the house a few weeks prior: Miss Hawthorne. She wore a stunning, shimmering black gown that hugged every curve; the two of them looked quite the pair. With her long dark hair cascading down her back in gentle waves, I thought she reminded me of someone, but I couldn't place who exactly.

Miss Hawthorne was right up against Leo, her hand on his chest, giggling as she flirted with him quite ostentatiously. Leo listened to her speak, giving her a polite smile, clearly not very interested in the story she was telling, but he made no attempt to brush her off or put distance between the two of them.

I heard Adam's voice in my head: "Don't be so petty—men are allowed to be friends with other women."

The fact that watching them together made me feel even a hint of animosity made me immediately insecure. I didn't want to be the Penny I had been with Adam. I couldn't go back there. And Leo had given me zero reason to believe he'd do anything like that—in fact he'd more than proven to me that he was much more mature, considerate, and kind than Adam was ever capable of being.

Still, watching the two of them interact made me uneasy. She was the type of woman he belonged with, from the right circles, the right family, the right kind of wealth. I merely worked for him.

Interrupting my downward spiral, Margot gently tapped on the microphone, signaling the party to quiet so she could give her speech with everyone's full attention.

Margot began by sharing an anecdote about her and George from when they'd been kids, trying to demonstrate how charity had always been something he had been fond of, painting him as a saint and conveniently showcasing herself in the same light.

She then went on to describe how the charity benefiting from donations that night, one that helped entrepreneurs and small business owners in third world countries, was so dear to George's heart and how it only felt right that this now-annual event be part of his legacy.

Margot pulled out a piece of paper at the end to offer words of appreciation to those who had donated for the gala, went out of their way to attend, and lastly, the few who helped her plan the event. There was one name mentioned that caught me off guard, the last of her list of helpers.

"And I would be remiss not to finally acknowledge my co-chair, Quinn Hawthorne." Margot smiled, her eyes meeting Quinn's, still at the bar, sidled up next to Leo, even closer than before.

My blood ran cold.

Miss Hawthorne was Quinn—Leo's Quinn—his ex.

"Quinn and I met a few years ago. She's helped me through a tremendous amount of challenges in my life and has been wise beyond her years in the advice and comfort she's given me. I'm so glad that she's found a lifelong partner in my nephew, her fiancé, Leo West. George would be so proud of the bright future you'll share together. Cheers!" Margot held up her glass of champagne, and the crowd applauded.

I felt like I was going to be sick.

I looked back to the bar, but Leo and Quinn were gone.

I needed to talk to Leo.

It couldn't be true—Margot had to be mistaken, or

maybe it had been wishful thinking on her part, that they would get back together.

He wouldn't do that to me…would he?

I frantically searched the ballroom with no luck. Feeling the panic rising, I sought out somewhere I could be alone, just for a moment, to calm down.

I ended up sitting in the bathroom for twenty minutes, focusing on my breathing to try to relax, although it was a rather pointless exercise. My head was spinning from the champagne and the dark thoughts winding their way through me along with the alcohol.

Knowing I couldn't hide forever and that I needed to find a way to ask Leo what was going on, to give him the opportunity to explain, I eventually returned to the ballroom. But once again, Margot intercepted me.

"I've been looking everywhere for you, darling," she purred.

She took a beat, looking me up and down, then said, "Are you alright? Have you had too much champagne?"

Maybe it was the alcohol, maybe it was my anxiety, or my patience wearing thin, but without thinking, I said, "I didn't know Miss Hawthorne was Quinn."

Margot turned her head. "I'm sorry," she apologized. "When I realized you didn't know who she was, I thought it was best not to mention it—Leo should have said something."

"He did say something—he told me that he broke off their engagement last year." My words came out defensively, despite my best efforts.

"That's what he said?" She raised a brow. "It's true that they hit a rough patch when Leo first returned to Willowbrooke. Adjusting to a long-distance relationship, and George's condition, was difficult for both of them. But Quinn moved back during the summer, and they decided to give it another shot since she was closer. She was of great comfort to Leo as he grieved."

I felt my heart sink. Why would Margot lie to me about something so serious? But more importantly, why would Leo keep it from me—and not just keep it from me, but actively lie about it? "Why haven't I seen her around the house—if they're together?" I swallowed, trying to find some shred of dignity to hang on to.

"Before you moved in, she was over all the time after working to set up the gallery and on the weekends. She felt uncomfortable after you started staying at Willowbrooke. But it's really none of your business—you're just Leo's interior designer. You should be happy for him to have found a second chance at love."

The cacophony of the music and conversation began to fade from my ears. I could feel how shallow my breathing was becoming, and I knew if I didn't sit down, I would pass out, an embarrassment I couldn't take, given the circumstances.

"Thank you, if you'll excuse me..." I gently squeezed Margot's hand to indicate I would be taking my leave, before turning on my heel to find an open seat out of her eyesight.

But before I had the chance, I spotted Leo tucked away in a booth at the back of the room, with Quinn in his lap. The two of them were all over each other.

"This can't be happening…" I whispered, blinking back the tears welling in my eyes. I couldn't cry in front of these people. I wouldn't.

Changing course, I exited the ballroom, stumbling out into the lobby.

"Do you have any available rooms?" I asked a woman working the front desk. I fumbled through my clutch for a credit card—I knew it was going to cost a fortune, but I certainly wasn't going back to Willowbrooke. "Please…" I felt a tear escape and quickly wiped it away.

"I just need an ID and a credit card," the woman replied sympathetically, taking the cards from me as I slid them across the counter.

Definitely drunk and positively devastated, I made the ridiculous decision to call William once I was alone in my hotel room. The call went to voicemail, but that didn't stop me from leaving a humiliating message, needing to cry to someone, and too cowardly to call Mina for some reason.

"Did you know?" I asked William over voicemail. "Did you know he was still with Quinn? You could have said something—but instead you encouraged me—pushed us together. He's here with her tonight—Margot said the engagement is back on and has been since this summer. You could have saved me all this heartache. I thought you were kinder than that—I shouldn't have called—sorry…" I hung up the phone.

The room was spinning.

I switched off the light and curled up on the bed, unable to stop the tears…

It was just before one in the morning when I awoke with a start to the trill of my phone ringing. I'd slept for just over two hours. Still a little buzzed, I answered the call without thinking or looking at the caller ID. "Hello?" I croaked.

"Jesus, Penny, I've been trying to get a hold of you for hours." William sounded worried. "What is going on?"

"I shouldn't have called you." I felt my face heat with embarrassment. "I've had too much to drink," I told him honestly.

"Is Leo alright? Is he with you?" William demanded.

"No—he's with Quinn…" I scowled, blinking back a fresh round of tears.

"Wait—what? I thought your voicemail—I didn't think you were serious," William stuttered. "What happened?"

I took a deep breath, willing myself to sober up. "During her speech, Margot said they were still engaged. She told me they've been together this whole time."

"That's not possible—he is *not* with Quinn—they ended things right after he came home to take care of George—last fall, I think."

"I saw them together at the bar—and later—they were kissing." I could feel bile rising in my throat at the thought of it…and probably because of the champagne.

"Penny, I'm telling you, something is wrong here. He's not with Quinn. He's in love with you—he told me so himself."

"What? But Margot said—"

"Quinn Hawthorne is just as much of a harpy as her benefactor, Margot West. I don't care what she said. I talked with Leo at length after their breakup, and I can assure you he would never even entertain the idea of reconciling with Quinn. He's made it quite clear to me that he has intentions to pursue you. I don't know what you saw, but something isn't right. And I can't get a hold of Leo either." William's usually professional demeanor had been replaced with true concern.

I felt a familiar pit of dread in my stomach. He was right. Whatever I had seen—it hadn't been like Leo. And if Leo wasn't answering his phone—maybe there was something wrong.

Then, as if hit by a truck, I had two astonishing revelations at once.

The first was that I knew why I'd recognized Quinn at the bar, with her long hair—she was the woman in the nightgown I'd seen walking across the lawn late that night. Her hair had been up the day she'd come to the house, and I hadn't seen her face in the darkness, but I knew it was her.

The second epiphany was related to something William

had said: Margot West. She'd introduced herself to me as Margot Collins—her married name. "Margot West—M W, not W M—she was the person Christine wrote about in her journal. She had killed her parents, and then Christine, when she found out. And I don't know how, but she probably killed George too," I told William, after explaining what I'd pieced together.

"Jesus…" he breathed, shocked at the epiphany. "Should I call the police?"

"I—I don't know," I stammered. "I have to go back to Willowbrooke. If Leo's not there—I don't—"

"I'll see if I can track his phone—I'll meet you there as soon as I can, but I'm a ways out of town," William told me. "And for heaven's sake, Penny, be careful."

CHAPTER 12
BAIT & SWITCH

Despite the lingering effects of the champagne, the couple hours of sleep and a quick trip to the bathroom prior to leaving my room all helped me feel more aware and in control with each passing moment.

It took longer than I'd hoped to secure a taxi to Willowbrooke, but the same front desk clerk that had helped me get a room was kind enough to call a few services before finally getting one to show up.

The driver was suspicious when I asked him to turn off his headlights as we approached the house, but did as I requested. And I couldn't have been more grateful, as the only lights in the house were coming from small gaps in the solarium's curtains.

Something was definitely wrong.

I didn't have a key to the house because I had never needed one before, but sometimes Carl forgot to lock the garage, and I was lucky enough that when he'd worked on the yard the day before, it had been one of those times.

I removed my heels before entering the house, not wanting to make too much noise. I didn't know what I was walking into, so I preferred to be cautious. If Margot really was responsible for killing multiple members of her family, there was no telling what else she was capable of.

Silently and carefully, I made my way through the dark house. I could hear Margot talking when I made it past the kitchen. Rather than going directly for the main door to the solarium, I slipped into Leo's bedroom, deciding to approach through the jack-and-jill bathroom instead. I briefly entertained the thought of changing into something other than an evening gown, but the closer I got, the more my heart started to race.

I knew Leo was in danger, and there was simply no time to waste.

Painfully slowly, I opened the door between the solarium and the bathroom, just a sliver, so I could see a bit of the room and hear Margot more clearly. What I saw sent a wave of panic coursing through every inch of my body.

Leo was lying on his father's hospital bed. His eyes were open, following Margot as she ranted at him about being ignored by her family during her childhood, but he wasn't moving. Had she paralyzed him? Drugged him?

The latter could explain what had happened with Quinn. There was no way she wasn't complicit in some way.

I felt an immediate and deep pang of guilt that I hadn't given him the benefit of the doubt, that I hadn't confronted him, so that I would have seen that he wasn't himself before it escalated to the level it had. Instead I had let my insecurities over my last relationship blind me, and I had chosen to drown my sorrows and feelings of inadequacies at the bottom of multiple champagne flutes.

My guilt was disrupted by a shock of temporary relief when I could have sworn that Leo made eye contact with me, peering through the crack in the bathroom door. I could have imagined it; it was pitch-dark in the bathroom. At least he was conscious, but then I saw something in Margot's hand catch the light, and my heart sank even further—it was a gun.

In a brief moment of clarity, I pulled out my phone. My fingers felt leaden as I struggled to text William: "Margot hurt Leo. She has a gun. Call the police. Hurry."

Fumbling with the phone, I remembered using a voice recording app to sometimes record meetings at the firm if I needed to send out notes afterwards. I found the app and started recording, placing my phone on the ground, wedged between the door and its frame, the microphone pointed toward the room.

As quietly as I could manage, I began to look through the bathroom drawers and cabinets for a weapon I could wield, while I allowed myself to tune in to Margot's mad ravings at Leo.

"You understand why I have to do this, right? I'll make it look like suicide—I'll lose the life insurance payout, but that almost makes it more credible. On top of your heartbroken stray, it will make sense that you couldn't handle the pressure of it all after so much loss."

Margot's strategy was, unfortunately, more sound than I could have hoped for. I'd fallen right into her trap, believing her over Leo, and giving her the opportunity to drag him back here. But her narcissism was also going to be her downfall, if I had anything to say about it.

Her need to explain the masterstrokes of her supposedly foolproof plan would be safely saved on my phone. She wasn't going to get away with any of it. I just needed to figure out how to get Leo out of the room unharmed, and I could deal with Margot later.

"Daddy was grooming me to be his successor—George didn't care about anything but himself. But then I found out he was still planning to leave everything to him! And why? Because he's a man." Margot paced around the solarium, still wearing her gown from the gala.

"I was stupid to think that George would give me my fair

share outright, looking back, but I was young, and I trusted him. I thought he'd be glad that Daddy got what he deserved. I hadn't intended to have to take care of Mommy too, but she was too suspicious, and she favored George as well—she was part of the problem. So I had to get her before she could turn me in.

"But then I met Ted, and at the beginning, things were so good. I had money of my own, so I wasn't worried about George being selfish. I knew Ted would take care of me. And then Christine had to come along and ruin everything." Margot rounded the bed and took a seat on the end, moving Leo's limp body to accommodate her.

His fearful eyes continued to follow her every move.

"Your mother and I were best friends for a time. She shared everything with me. We'd have the best time gallivanting around town. Being a housewife and mother bored her to tears. But I got sloppy and shared a little too much with her after one drink too many. I'll admit, I didn't think she was smart enough to put the pieces together, but then I found her diary one day, and there it was, on paper, that she was getting ready to go to the police.

"My life would have been ruined. George would have disowned me. Ted would never have forgiven me. I saw her walking near the cliff the next day, and I don't know what came over me. I just—pushed her." Margot smiled as if recalling a nice memory, rather than a murder. "It was easier than I'd thought—certainly easier than the others. She was just there one minute and gone the next. Simple." Margot laughed humorlessly.

"Things were good for years after that. I was happy with Ted, until he started cheating on me—keeping things from me. He left the country before I could do anything about it—cut me off financially—made me look like a fool—that bastard.

"George helped me—let me move into the cottage. But being back at Willowbrooke, not having a penny to my name without a man's signature, just reminded me that my legacy had been stolen from me," she spat bitterly, getting up again to continue pacing.

"When he got cancer, I thought my prayers had been answered. He'd told me years before he was going to cut you out of the will—wanted you to make your own money. I would be set. I just had to wait him out. But then one night, over drinks, he told me he'd changed his mind and didn't want to disinherit you. I was going to lose everything for good.

"But I came up with a plan. I thought if I could lure you back here, that George would be reminded why the two of you had fallen out in the first place. You reminded him so much of Christine—but he only wanted her. He never wanted a child—she did. He gave her a baby to keep her happy, and then when she was gone, you were this awful reminder that he'd never get her back. He was never meant to be a father—but he sure liked the idea of having an heir—

typical man, wanting his line to be carried on.

"What I hadn't expected was for you to show up and prove to him how you'd grown—how you'd matured. I didn't think he'd be impressed with your business—become fond of you, after all those years he kept you at arm's length. I suppose that was an error—to underestimate your charm and humility. Both of those traits definitely came from your mother. There isn't a West in existence who was either of those things.

"And when you broke up with Quinn—that poor girl—I think that sealed it. George saw you making decisions for yourself, not for others, and I knew I'd made a mistake bringing you back. My inheritance would be stolen from me again."

Margot walked to the window, peering out into the darkness, before returning to Leo's side.

"The nurse wasn't hard to convince; she had debts. And it was easy to set it up to make William look like a potential suspect. Getting rid of her last week was a bit more challenging; however, I have a far-reaching network of contacts. But George—" Margot shook her head. "That asshole had one last card up his sleeve—he'd never changed the will in the first place like he'd told me. You were always the only person to inherit everything. All my plans—and I was still penniless.

"And speaking of pennies…she was a complication I didn't see coming."

I froze at the mention of my name. Having searched the

bathroom top to bottom, albeit in the dark, the best weapon I could find was a pair of scissors. It would have to do—the next best thing was a curling iron. I made my way closer to the door, listening more intently, trying to formulate some kind of plan of action for how to disarm Margot.

The bed was on wheels, but no doubt the brakes were engaged. I wouldn't have time to drag Leo into the bathroom and lock both doors. I wasn't sure that I'd be able to get a swing at Margot before she got a shot off at me, or worse, Leo.

"At first I was resigned to thinking I might be able to manipulate you into turning everything over to me—you were so broken after losing this man that was a father to you in name only." She spat the words, as if him having any kind of affection for his father was nothing but a weakness, even though she was guilty of the same crime. "But then you started spending his money without abandon to restore the house like George wanted. At the rate you were going, I wasn't sure I'd have an inheritance left.

"And Penny—that stupid girl." Margot shook her head. "Leo, rule number one: you don't fuck the help—I thought you knew better. And the two of you, thinking you could keep it a secret from me, while you follow her around moon-faced. How convenient for her to lose her housing so she'd have to stay here." Margot threw her hands in the air.

"You know she's taking you for a ride, right? It's always the same with people like her. You thought Quinn wanted your money? Well at least Quinn comes from a good family, and has funding of her own. She would have been a good match—marriage is like business. You don't understand that you should find a partner that brings something to the table. What does that girl have? Nothing," Margot spat.

"I will give her credit for finding Christine's journal. I should have known to check the library—it was an oversight, but I got it back easily enough. She didn't want George to know that we were friends—he thought I had a bad influence on her—I imagine that's why she used that little code for me. Me? A bad influence? She was lucky I took her under my wing."

"Did you know the pink room was mine growing up?" Margot asked Leo, who was incapable of responding. "There's a false back to the closet that leads to the green room next door. I did try to scare Penny away. It was too easy to sneak up from the basement and torment her. Of course I didn't realize I'd be chasing her right into your welcoming arms, dear nephew." She rolled her eyes. "You could have avoided all this heartbreak if she'd just heeded my warnings. Maybe I should have tried to scare her a bit more seriously." Margot laughed.

But Margot's laugh was interrupted by a chirp coming from my phone.

I stared down at the device in horror, and I knew this was my one chance to do something—anything.

I heard Margot stomp toward the door before yanking

it open, at which time I seized the opportunity to lunge at Margot, knocking her off her feet. The gun clattered to the ground, landing near Leo in the hospital bed.

My phone skittered across the floor as a result, and as it passed her, she realized with terror that I had been recording her.

We both clambered for the phone. It had all the evidence needed to put her away. Whoever got to the phone first would decide her fate. Unfortunately, it was Margot who reached it. Grabbing it from the ground, she pushed past me and took off running.

Briefly, my eyes met Leo's. They were wide in terror.

I looked down, the gun catching my attention as its polished metal shone in the light. Without thinking, I picked it up and gave chase, following Margot as she headed for the basement.

Margot thundered down the stairs, well ahead of me. It was pitch-black, and I didn't have the time or thought to turn on any lights, I just ran on instinct. I knew where she was going—the tunnels. It seemed so obvious now; of *course* they led to the cottage.

I could hear Margot's frantic breathing in the dark as we stumbled through the dank air, past stone walls. As I pursued her, I thought of the gun in my hand. I'd never used a gun before—I'd only seen them used on TV or in movies.

But I recognized the part of the gun I needed to cock in order to engage it. I knew there was likely a safety switch, but having never held one before, I didn't know where it was, or how to unlock it, so if it wasn't already off, I'd be sunk. I had no faith in my aim—or in having the courage to actually pull the trigger, but perhaps adrenaline alone would assist me in such a feat.

Not having thought through the logistics of chasing Margot, I realized with alarm as I emerged on the other side of the tunnel that I had no idea what part of the cottage I'd be entering, and in the darkness, Margot had the upper hand in all matters. And sure enough, suddenly the wind was knocked out of me as Margot barreled into me from the side, the moment I made it out of the tunnel.

Wheezing, some of my vision returned as a singular sconce illuminated the storage room under Margot's house. I'd never been down there before.

I looked around and spotted the gun a few feet from Margot. I propelled myself for the weapon, but Margot was too close. We struggled over the gun, and in the process, it fired.

Guess the safety wasn't on after all.

I felt the blood along my side before searing pain ripped through me. It had only grazed me, though. But Margot had already won. In one hand, she still held my phone, and in the other, the gun—pointed directly at me.

"YOU RUINED EVERYTHING!" Margot screeched. "I was just fighting for what belonged to me, what was taken from me—my birthright!" Her hands trembled as she considered if she should end me. "You should understand. Your parents were the same—marginalizing you."

Still catching my breath, I could only watch and listen. Even if I had been capable of speaking, I knew it would only enrage her further. Like a true egomaniac, she needed it to be about her; she needed to be understood—to be in control. And she was completely out of control—she was spiraling.

"You never should have come here…" She shook her head, regaining some sort of composure.

And I knew at that moment I was done for.

She cocked the gun.

I closed my eyes, feeling tears falling on my cheeks. I hoped that William would make it in time to save Leo.

Margot pulled the trigger.

I flinched.

But the gun only made a clicking noise.

It was jammed!

Before she could try again, there was a thud upstairs, which took her attention from me. She looked toward the staircase, where police had begun to stream into the basement.

Click. Click. Click.

She tried firing at them. But the gun was still stuck.

"Hands up—drop the gun!" one of the police yelled.

As if in slow motion, I watched as one of the officers tackled Margot to the ground in her soiled evening gown when she refused to comply.

After that, everything went black.

EPILOGUE

"You got a real Christmas tree!?" Mina exclaimed, barreling through the door, kicking her shoes off before she ran to the tree Leo had surprised me with a couple weeks before. "It smells so nice!" she exclaimed, examining the lights, tinsel, and vintage ornaments Leo had unearthed from the basement, where the prohibition tunnels had been safely blocked off.

"We never got a real one growing up." I smiled, following her into the living room.

"Me neither." Mina glanced back at me before her attention shifted to the larger room. "Wow, Pen, you really outdid yourself here." She took a couple minutes to slowly wander around the open living room and into the kitchen, inspecting the craftsmanship and little details. "You'd put some of the senior designers at my company to shame." She shook her head.

"Really?" I felt a blush creep along my cheeks; that was a compliment I hadn't expected to receive. It meant a lot coming from her—she was honest to a fault with me.

Mina nodded earnestly. "I know I'm biased, being your best friend and all, but I can't believe you did all this yourself."

"Well Leo helped, and Danny, the lead contractor—"

"Penny." Mina stopped me. "Acknowledge your accomplishments." She reminded me of the mantra she had learned in therapy and passed along to me somewhere along the way.

"Thank you, Mina." I smiled bashfully. "Lunch is ready, if you're hungry." I motioned to the takeout containers on the counter. "You said this was your favorite in the area."

"You are so thoughtful." She squeezed my arm as she passed me to make herself a plate. "And where is the dashing Leo West today?"

I shook my head, taking a seat at a barstool. "Said he had some business in town."

Mina's shoulders slumped. "I was ready to grill him about his intentions."

I couldn't help but laugh. If he happened to return before we finished lunch, he'd be in for quite the interrogation. "Another time, perhaps."

"I'll settle for you telling me every minute detail of what

you've done to redesign this space." She grinned from ear to ear, eager for me to complete the request.

"Twist my arm," I joked sarcastically before launching into a full postmortem of the specifics of the process, planning, and execution for the entirety of the project.

There were, after all, only minor details left to complete, a delayed purchase here and there, or random bits, like a living room side table lamp which Leo had been picky about, wanting to wait until he found one he felt was perfect for the space.

"And what about you, Penny?" Mina hedged. "Now that you're an action hero with a legit scar from an actual bullet…" She joked, but the question was serious.

"Better," I simpered, unsure of how to share the full breadth of how I was feeling a month later.

After the police found Margot and me, things were still quite a blur. I remembered waking up in the hospital room, where Leo was waiting at my side, having recovered from the Rohypnol Quinn had slipped in his drink, leaving him half-conscious and practically paralyzed under its control.

He remembered nothing after his first cocktail at the gala and was beyond horrified when I recounted the events of the evening from my point of view.

"You have to know—I would never…" Leo had choked, holding my hand across the hospital bed.

"I do now—I'm sorry I didn't then. Margot plied me with so much champagne—"

"I don't care—just so long as you know now—sober, that I couldn't do that to you," he pleaded, as if it was somehow his fault for what Quinn and Margot had done to him.

"Leo—"

"I love you, Penny," he blurted out, holding back tears from guilt over something he didn't remember, something that hadn't been his doing at all.

"I love you too," I replied with a watery smile, squeezing his hand to let him know that we were okay.

After being discharged from the hospital the next day with dressings over the gash at my side and multiple doctors telling me how lucky I'd been that it hadn't been a millimeter this way or that, Leo had doted on me back at the house, afraid to leave my side for more than a couple minutes at a time, before I had to gently let him know that I was okay, and while his smothering was sweet, that he didn't need to hover.

Margot was behind bars while awaiting her trial, having been denied bail because she was not only a flight risk, but also a danger to the community, according to the appointed judge. Leo's lawyer was worried she might try to plead insanity, but assured us that even if she succeeded, she'd still be under lock and key.

"There may be some benefits to a sentence at an institution versus a correctional facility for someone like Margot, but considering the lifestyle she's used to, either will be just as bad," the lawyer had commented.

Thankfully, the DA decided my quick thinking in

recording Margot's unhinged villainous manifesto toward Leo was more than enough for a conviction. But Quinn had also turned on Margot and would be a witness for the prosecution, in exchange for a lesser sentence—likely only probation, according to Leo's lawyer, because of her connections. Leo wasn't nearly as worried about Quinn as he was about Margot, but he got a restraining order against her just to be safe.

Most of the time, it felt like a bad dream, but sometimes, a visceral memory would unleash itself, shaking me to my core for a split second. It would be enough to send me reeling for a while, having to focus on my breathing and remind myself I was safe.

Even my parents reached out after hearing what had happened. Of course they brushed off the lapse in communication like it was nothing and instead probed me about my relationship with Leo.

Once again, I found myself disappointed in them. But with Leo's support and so much on the horizon, I found it hard to let that disappointment bring me down.

Things went quite differently with Sloan.

Over an emotional visit, she tearfully explained how the thought of coming so close to losing me had made her realize how bad she felt about the state of our relationship. It wasn't just how we had been constantly pitted against each other, but how we'd both used that as an excuse to keep our distance, even as adults.

"Do you think we can start over? Is that even possible?" She'd held my hands across the kitchen counter. "I feel like we've wasted so much time, and I miss you."

Her confession was sobering, but I found I felt the same way. "I'll always be your sister," I told her, squeezing her hands in mine.

Things had been nice between us since then. Mostly brief texts and the occasional meme about narcissistic parents, but it was more of a connection than we'd had years. I felt optimistic about forging a new kind of relationship with her—one that was on our own terms.

I threw myself into completing work on the house, trying to keep my mind off everything that had happened that night. The kitchen was completely done, the flooring refinished through the entirety of the home, the library reorganized and cataloged, and all bedrooms and bathrooms updated.

Willowbrooke was pristine.

She was, quite simply, my masterpiece.

I didn't know how I was ever going to top this project.

Leo was a very welcome distraction as well. And although the image of him with Quinn would occasionally plague me, I found myself thinking of it less and less the closer Leo and I became.

Still disappointed that she had missed Leo, Mina and I eventually said our goodbyes, agreeing to another lunch date after the new year. Eager to get home to her own partner and spend Christmas Eve with his family, we lingered in the entryway in a tight hug.

"I'm glad you're safe," she whispered. "I'm glad you're happy."

I pulled her even closer. "Thank you."

And with that, she was gone. My heart was always so full after spending time with her. I was still so distracted by thoughts of our conversation and her enthusiasm over how the house had turned out, that I didn't hear Leo saunter in near dinnertime. He startled me when he gave me a soft kiss at my temple before dropping a bag of groceries on the counter.

"Everything alright?"

I nodded, changing the subject before he had time to probe further. "You sure you want to cook?" I had hoped we could relax together, and there were plenty of leftovers from lunch.

But cooking was one of the ways Leo relaxed, so I relented when he insisted.

"Can I help?" I offered instead.

"Sure." He smiled, pointing to vegetables that needed to be rinsed and diced.

Working seamlessly together, we danced around each other in the kitchen in silence, until I couldn't bear it any longer.

"What were you up to today?" I tried to keep my tone light, but hiding my curiosity was impossible. Leo wasn't terribly secretive with me about anything, certainly not since the incident with Margot. He was now an open book—which was beyond refreshing.

Leo laughed, but didn't respond.

"Mina thought you might be avoiding her," I suggested.

"I would never avoid the Spanish Inquisition," he joked. "I was asking William's advice on a new business venture." Finally he answered my initial question. I thought perhaps only to avoid more of my badgering over him conveniently being out of the house during Mina's visit.

"Oh." I was surprised by his answer. I noticed Leo had become increasingly antsy now that the major house work had been completed, and wondered if perhaps it was because he was rudderless without work to focus on, but I hadn't mentioned my suspicions to him yet.

"I've been waiting for the right thing to come along, and I think I've found it." He remained cryptic.

"And William agrees?"

Leo nodded. "He loves it, actually."

I smiled at the thought of Leo finding something more fulfilling to do with his time. "You're not going to share?" I nudged him, careful to do so when he wasn't holding a knife.

He smirked. "Not yet."

I narrowed my eyes at him, but allowed him to get away with the transgression, knowing he wouldn't keep it from me for long, and likely had a good reason for doing so.

"So how did lunch with Mina go?"

"She loves the house." I couldn't help but grin,

remembering her kind words.

"Of course she does—anyone who doesn't love what you've done clearly has no taste." Leo spoke so matter-of-factly, it made me blush. As if I was some famous designer who'd been in business for years working for the rich and famous, not Penny Abbot, with a singular professional project to my name.

"Thank you." I rubbed my palm against the small of his back while he worked.

"Speaking of the house, we need to start talking about the exterior work so we're ready to go in the spring." He began to throw the cut-up ingredients into a pan, masterfully tossing the vegetables as he sauteed them, a skill that was both impressive and well beyond where my cooking abilities would ever be.

"I didn't realize you wanted to start work outside so soon—I thought I'd start looking for a place as close as possible within my budget." I hadn't mentioned it to him before, but I didn't want to wear out my welcome in his home.

Leo stopped abruptly and turned to me. "What are you talking about?"

I froze, unsure how to respond.

"You want to—to move out?" he stuttered.

"I just figured when the work was complete, you wouldn't want…"

I stopped when Leo's expression became a mixture of

bewilderment and anxiety.

"Do you want to move out?" he repeated himself.

"No."

Leo released an exasperated breath, then made eye contact with me again. "Please don't look for an apartment."

"Okay." I winced as I instinctively added, "I'm sorry."

Leo paused again, wrapping his arms around me, pulling me into a hug, letting the food crackle on the stove. "I want you here," he said simply, before kissing my temple and returning to the frying pan.

"Besides"—his tone returned to its naturally jovial state— "if you would have bothered to read the updated contract you signed last month, you would have noticed there was a clause that stipulated you have guaranteed housing while you're working on the estate."

"Oh, remind me to send any future paperwork you give me to my nonexistent lawyer," I retorted.

"I will," he jested.

I was surprised at the immediate flood of relief that washed over me, knowing that I could stay with him…that he wanted me to stay. I hadn't realized until that moment, but since Margot was safely situated behind bars, Willowbrooke had begun to feel like home. Leo had always felt that way, but the house had resisted me—or rather, Margot had made it feel that way.

So I had convinced myself over the last few weeks that it would be best if I assumed I would be asked to leave when the project was complete. I had been protecting myself—taking action before the other shoe could drop.

There was still a part of me that remained guarded… the last vestiges of my relationship with Adam and the disappointment and shame that radiated from being with him for so long. But hearing Leo say that he wanted me—that he wanted me to stay…I felt the last bits of whatever wall was left crumbling.

After dinner, we made our way over to the living room, like most other nights, wineglasses in hand, cuddling up next to each other on the couch, enjoying the light of the fire and the tree as much as each other's company.

"So now that your stay has been extended indefinitely—"

"Indefinitely?" I raised a brow; I hadn't realized he was that serious, but it secretly made me warm to think about remaining at Willowbrooke, with him, without some looming deadline hanging over me.

"Yes," he said firmly. "Indefinitely."

I giggled at his indignance, taking a sip of my wine.

"Is there anything you'd change?"

"We've barely finished." I laughed.

"I know, but I'm asking—as the lady of the house—"

I just about spit out my wine at that comment.

Leo narrowed his eyes at me, but there was a glimmer of humor behind them. "Now that this is your home, is there anything you would change?"

"It's your home," I countered teasingly.

Leo pursed his lips. "It's just as much yours as mine. Now answer the question."

"Well…" I took a moment to think. "We might consider moving to the upstairs master. It has an ensuite and much more closet space."

"Turn our room back into a study?" His use of "our" was not lost on me.

I nodded.

"Then you'd have an office," he offered.

I laughed, because why would it be mine? "Or it could be your office."

"Or we could share," Leo compromised.

I snorted a laugh. "Like I would get any work done if we shared an office."

"Why is that?" Leo raised an eyebrow. He knew exactly why, he just wanted to hear me say it out loud.

I refused.

But the blush creeping across my cheeks was more than enough to give me away.

"You naughty little thing," Leo snickered, nuzzling against me.

I shoved him, rolling my eyes when he feigned an injury.

"So what else? What else are we editing?" He smiled impishly as he sipped his wine.

There was one last thing, though I was apprehensive to mention it.

But Leo seemingly already knew. "Just say it," he

commanded, eyes still twinkling.

I glared at him, but didn't reply.

"The solarium?" he guessed correctly.

I remained silent.

"I know," he sighed, finally letting the facade falter.

"I wasn't so much thinking of redecorating as I was thinking about rebranding." I tried to spin my idea to seem more appealing.

My plan worked. Leo quirked a brow, curious at what I had in mind.

"What if it wasn't the solarium, but rather, a conservatory," I proposed. "We could fill it with plants, comfy furniture, and a telescope for stargazing."

I stopped, surprised by Leo's wide grin. "I love it."

"Really?" I asked earnestly.

"Can I tell you a secret?" he said conspiratorially, his voice low as he leaned forward.

I nodded slowly.

"I'd agree to any changes you wanted to make, as long as it meant you were staying."

Careful not to spill my wine, I gently wound my arm around Leo's neck and pulled him to me. He always seemed to know exactly what pace I required. His lips were slow and soft, lightly pressing and tugging…he had become an expert at unwinding the tight coil inside me.

When a quiet whimper escaped me, he pulled back. "We

should go to the room," he breathed against my skin, unable to separate himself any farther.

"We could just stay out here," I murmured, placing soft kisses along his jaw. I didn't want to move. I wanted him right where he was.

"Santa won't come if we sleep in the living room." Leo managed to unwind my arm from around him, and took my wineglass from me.

I narrowed my eyes at Leo. We'd discussed this weeks ago. "Santa better not be coming, because we agreed no presents," I threatened.

Leo chuckled. "I feel like I should make some kind of innuendo about our precise use of words."

"Leo…" I warned.

He sighed, removing himself from beneath me as he stood. "Come to bed."

"You promised," I pouted. I hadn't gotten him anything. And I knew whatever he had done would be over the top and expensive, and something I had no chance of reciprocating, even if I had bought him a gift.

"It's not what you think." He extended his hand and helped me from the couch, then led me down the hall to the bedroom.

My brow furrowed as I tried to parse his words.

"Don't be upset all night," he whispered before kissing me again, then tugging my shirt over my head. "Give me the benefit of the doubt."

"Leo…" But the indignance in my voice turned into a moan when his fingers slipped below the elastic of my panties.

He was distracting me.

I wasn't strong enough to argue when I wanted to give in so badly.

Skin against skin, any lingering anger or annoyance with Leo for definitely going back on our deal left me as his body rocked against me. The building climax between us was enough to make anyone forget themselves.

I fell asleep to whispered vows of love and adoration, tucked into Leo's side, cozy under the covers.

Waking up the next morning, I sighed, feeling the emptiness of Leo's side of the bed. I had hoped for a slow, sleepy lovemaking session before breakfast. But the smell of strong coffee permeating the closed bedroom door dashed that plan.

I threw on Leo's discarded sweatshirt from the day before, hoping that I might still be able to persuade him to come back to bed with my bare legs, a trick that usually worked.

Hearing Leo rummaging around in the storage room behind the kitchen, I glanced at the tree, letting out a sigh of relief when I saw that it was still empty. But I had been too quick to jump to conclusions, because as I turned back to the kitchen, there was a blue velvet box sitting on the counter.

My heart skipped a beat. My thoughts ran a mile a

minute.

It was too soon.

Wasn't it?

Did I want a ring?

A proposal?

What would Mina think?

What would my family say?

But as I approached, I realized the box was too big—or at least larger than a typical ring box, but perhaps too small for a necklace. Shit—a bracelet.

More thoughts raced through my mind.

How much had he spent?

Would I even be able to wear something so expensive?

I didn't question his taste, but would I like it?

Leo cleared his throat.

Caught up, I hadn't noticed him return to the kitchen, staring at me while I spiraled.

"Good morning, sweetheart." He laughed, clearly observing my crisis.

"Hi." I swallowed.

"It's not jewelry." He looked down at the box, then back up at me, before turning his attention to pouring me a cup of coffee.

I felt my spine relax at the admission as I warily approached the kitchen counter. "I thought we'd sleep in…" I tried to ignore the box.

Leo smirked, sliding the coffee mug across the counter,

past the gift. "We can go back to bed in a bit." His tone was suggestive, as I had hoped.

I took a large gulp of the warm, bitter liquid after taking a seat on a barstool.

"Are you going to open it?" Leo raised a brow.

I stared at him, not wanting to look down at the box. "You agreed—"

"Just open it, Pen." Leo laughed.

He'd said it wasn't jewelry. He'd thought the whole thing to be funny. Maybe it was just a gag gift. I took another sip of my coffee before giving in.

Within the box sat a single card, wedged between the folds of more of the same blue velvet fabric.

It read: Penny Abbot Designs

Immediately I felt tears welling in my eyes and a lump forming in my throat.

I picked up the card from the velvet box, examining it.

He had listed my cell phone, the address for Willowbrooke, it even had a website with my own business email address using the domain.

The design was simple and elegant. The cardstock was matte, textured, and thick. It was clear he'd put a lot of thought into it.

I loved it.

I couldn't comprehend how someone could know me so well when I had spent so long trying to hide myself from others. But I could never hide from Leo. He always found me.

I looked up at him again, through my tears, trying to put to words what I was feeling inside, but found the task impossible.

Leo West had been one of two people in my entire life to believe in me and to love me for exactly who I was without expectations.

But he had been the only one capable of giving me the opportunity to prove myself, to show my skills, to start my career, to live my dream, to feel loved unconditionally.

He had given me everything.

I felt him at my side as he took a seat on the stool next to me. I looked up at Leo, who produced a small cardboard box that I assumed contained the rest of the cards he had ordered. He set a binder down on the counter on his other side, still out of my view.

"You didn't have to do this," I whimpered, brushing away the tears that had begun to fall.

"I should have ordered them a long time ago," he replied, running his hand up and down my back, trying to comfort me. "I didn't mean to make you cry."

"They're happy tears," I protested. "I love it."

Leo chuckled before leaning in and giving me a kiss on the cheek.

"What's that?" I motioned to the binder.

Leo's eyes darted to the portfolio nervously. He took a deep breath as he slid it across the counter in front of me.

The cover used the same font and style as the card, but read: Penny Abbot Designs Business Plan.

Leo's hand found mine, and I looked up at him curiously. "This is what you were meeting with William about?" I asked.

Leo nodded. He was usually better at hiding his anxiety. Whatever he was about to say, he was scared. I waited patiently for him to speak.

"You know I've been thinking about what was next for a while. I knew it had to be a good fit— something more permanent." He paused. "You and I make a good team—at least I think we do," he fumbled.

I smiled at him, agreeing.

Thankful for the acknowledgement he continued. "What I really want to do is keep working with you," he admitted.

I couldn't stop my brow from rising at the revelation.

Leo swallowed, trying to maintain the courage to keep going. "I think we've been able to keep a good professional relationship, aside from our personal relationship—"

"They've both been pretty good," I encouraged him.

Leo smiled. "I was hoping you'd be interested in a joint-partnership." Having finally got to the part he was waiting for, he launched into full sales mode. "You could design your heart out, and I could bring in leads through my network, and run the business side. I have a ton of contacts I can leverage, and with my business acumen and your talent—"

"Yes," I interrupted him.

"Yes?" He blinked.

"Yes," I repeated.

"You don't need to hear the rest of the pitch?" he blanched, seemingly in shock that I had already agreed to his proposal.

To be fair, I was usually more argumentative and inquisitive. But I was so sure. I didn't hesitate, because it was right. For once in my life, it was all right. I didn't need time to consider his proposal.

"You can keep going if you like—but yes to all of it." I leaned forward and kissed Leo, unable to keep myself from moving closer to him. Leo cupped my cheek in his palm, letting his thumb gently stroke along my bottom lip, our foreheads together.

After a moment, I pulled back. "You're still in trouble for getting me a present," I joked, trying to lighten the mood.

Leo's face contorted into the widest grin I'd ever seen, before we broke down in a fit of giggles together.

"Well, you're still in trouble for thinking I was going to kick you out after the restoration—so maybe we can call it even," he suggested through more laughs.

"Alright." I pulled Leo in for another kiss.

"I love you," he whispered against my mouth.

"I love you, too."

Thank you for reading my debut novel, Willowbrooke!

If you enjoyed the book, it would mean the world to me if you would consider leaving a rating or review on Amazon, Goodreads, or the platform of your choice.

ACKNOWLEDGEMENTS

I'm not exactly sure when I started writing, but I've always had a very vivid imagination. I remember writing chapters of stories at night and sharing them with my friends on the school bus the next morning. I remember writing fan fiction in college and being so baffled but humbled that anyone would want to read anything I wrote, let alone enjoy it. I remember the group of girls that introduced me to NaNoWriMo when I moved to Los Angeles, over fifteen years ago. I remember the awe I felt after finishing my first novel; I was in sheer disbelief that I could create something like that. And I remember every single person who has supported me along the way.

For my mom, my greatest champion, who always taught me I could do anything, who encouraged me with all the kindness in her big heart, this book is for you.

For my dad and my brothers, who have bolstered all of my endeavors, and loved me the way they each knew how, this book is for you.

For Caitlin, who listens to me ramble for hours about

my ridiculous ideas and is always honest when she hates the character names I want to use, this book is for you.

For Amanda, Bre, and my Saturday writing group, who have become staples in my life and offer me the consistency, structure, and peace of mind I needed to realize I could publish this on my own, this book is for you.

For Heather, LL, Ashley, Halle, Sam and Emarie, who helped me make these words and their packaging look this brilliant, who offered kind words of support and feedback when I was scared, anxious, and overwhelmed trying to figure out how to navigate publishing this thing, this book is for you.

And finally, for my younger self, who always had a story in her heart, characters on her mind, and the dream of publishing one day, but who also harbored a million doubts about what she was capable of, wondered who on earth would want to read anything she wrote, or how it was possible she was good enough to publish something…to be vulnerable so very publicly, this book is for you. You did it. You're an author now. Nobody can take this from you. You are enough.

About the Author

AJ Wynn is a Southern California-based author who works in marketing professionally, but whose true passion lies in writing. Weaving captivating stories with romance, mystery, fantasy, and much more allows AJ to express her creativity and serves as a canvas for her boundless imagination. When not immersed in the world of words, AJ is an avid reader, book dragon, and interior decorating enthusiast. Her favorite cozy days are accompanied by a fresh cup of coffee and her faithful canine sidekick.

Stay up to date with AJ Wynn's latest releases:

🌐 **www.AJWynn.com**

⬜ **@AJWynnWrites**

🧵 **@AJWynnWrites**